ONE BILLION
REASONS

MILLIE BELIZAIRE

margate press

MARGATE PRESS

CONTENTS

PROLOGUE

<u>Damien</u>

We killed my mother together.

Well... the only mother I'd ever known. To anyone with eyes, it was obvious that Desiree wasn't my *real* mother, but she was as close to a mom as I ever had.

It was a cold night in January. I remember that night being cold because that kind of dip in temperature wasn't common for South Florida, even in January. At most, it might've been a good thirty-eight degrees outside.

Sometimes, when I close my eyes and travel back to that night, I can still feel the cold wet grass between my toes as I watched our white house burn to the ground. I can still smell the smoke rising up to fill the entire neighborhood.

And oftentimes, in my nightmares... I can still hear her screaming.

My father made me help him do it.

At the time, I just didn't know I was helping. Even now, I'm a little ashamed to admit that at fifteen, I still feared my father. If he told me to do something, I never really felt like I had a say in the matter.

We were coming up on the last weekend of Christmas break. It was the first Saturday of the new year and I woke up to shouting, which was normal in my house. When I took a look at my bedside clock, it was just a few minutes shy of three o'clock in the morning, which was *not* normal.

As a veteran police officer, Sergeant Joseph Fine kept a rigid schedule that forced everybody in the house to be quiet by nine o'clock. Unless kept up for work, he was rarely ever awake past midnight, and if you were the unlucky pair of feet that might wake him before six o'clock, you'd soon find yourself on your ass.

There were no late nights in this house. At least, there wasn't supposed to be.

"Desiree, if you don't *shut* the fuck up..."

My parents were fighting, and from the way that the sound traveled, the argument was coming from their bedroom. Dad's voice was muffled at first, like the argument was just beginning to boil. Desiree said something and I knew it set him off because that's when the shouting started.

I could sit for hours, trying to recall what the shouting was about, but it would slip through my fingers like dust every single time. All that I remember was that it was loud. Sometimes, my father's voice could be so overpowering that the air seemed to vibrate when he would shout. As much noise as he made that night, the actual words sound like TV static in my memories.

I just remember sitting up against the headboard in my dark bedroom to the sounds of my father going in on Desiree. I rubbed the tiredness out of my eyes as moonlight crept in from outside through the blinds, and I listened. It was his last threat that still echoes through time.

"If you don't stop all that crying, I swear I'll give you something to cry about."

Something in their room was thrown against the wall, shattering, I remember the sounds of tight fists hitting against skin, and finally the sound of a woman crying out.

"Joseph, I'm sorry!"

Then it was quiet.

Just another night of my father taking out his frustrations on Desiree's face, I thought. This was nothing new. Tomorrow morning, she would be in the kitchen, fixing breakfast as if we couldn't all see the new bruises on her skin. I was used to this. It had happened too many times for my stomach to twist into knots about it now.

I tried to go back to bed.

Of course, I wanted to be the type of person who could stick up for her. Though, back then, I wasn't much built for protecting anybody; not even myself. I was just a scrawny fifteen-year-old kid, quicker to pick up a pencil than to hold up a fist, an abuse victim in my own right. When Dad wasn't beating on her, I was usually his second choice.

There are people who make it their business to study the choices I made in those days. Most of them think they would've behaved differently in my shoes. *Why didn't he at least call the police?* The really naïve ones always ask that question.

My father *was* the police.

Most of the officers within a twenty-mile radius were some of my father's closest friends. Quiet as it's kept, a good number of those cops were beating on their wives, too.

So, I just had to try to drown out all the shouting.

Just as my head hit the pillow that night, right before my eyes could close, I heard heavy footsteps getting closer to my room. In my bed, I sat back up just as the door began to open and standing at the doorframe was my panting father. The hallway light nearly turned him into a shadow at the threshold, and he stood there with wild eyes, his shoulders sliding up and down like he just couldn't breathe enough.

I'd never seen him this frantic before.

He spoke before I could, trying to sound calm. "I need your help with something, Dame."

That's what he would call me when he was trying to be my friend. My real mother—his wife before Desiree—named me after his father because he told her to, and he wouldn't even call me that. Most days, I was just '*Boy*' and on the really bad days, I was '*Stupid*', but when he wanted something, I was Dame.

When I try to look back on this night, the images always come back choppy and incomplete. It doesn't play like a movie in my head; it comes to me like a compilation of different scenes, one after the other, sometimes out of order.

In my memories, one minute I'm in my bedroom, the next minute I'm standing in the living room with a five-gallon tank of gasoline hanging from my fingers. Dad held a smaller tank in his hands, emptying it out onto the pristine living room furniture.

That's when I knew things were about to go left.

Because that furniture was new. We had just bought that set of white leather couches at *City Furniture* two months ago. Everything in this house was new. We'd only been living here for about six weeks, and I watched as my father doused the house he'd been so proud of in gasoline.

When his tank had emptied, he looked at me and said, "I'm gonna go wake up your little brother, and you finish pouring that gas all throughout the house. Get every corner."

I hadn't asked any questions. My father wasn't exactly the type of man you *could* question. I was young, but I was a smart kid. I thought I figured it out on my own. It had been my assumption that the old man had just finally went too far and killed her, and that this little house fire was his way of covering it up.

When I told detectives that part of the story, they looked at me funny. How could I both learn and accept the death of my stepmother in the span of a single second? It was suspicious to them that I didn't cry enough. *So, you didn't like her?*

No—I loved her.

I know my behavior was strange and detached, but there are really no words for the way I felt that night. In my mind, Desiree had always been destined to die, and there was nothing I could do about it. To me, it had never been a question of *if* my father would be the one to kill her someday, just when. I always knew he would. So, while I was devastated, I had already mourned Desiree years in advance.

Whether I showed it or not, that night I was a mess of emotions that had no business being mixed together. They mixed together so strangely that it all fed back as numbness. Grieving, angry, nauseated, defenseless, and terrified.

Especially that last one.

Terrified that I might be next if I didn't do as I was told.

So, I took that five-gallon cannister of gasoline and used it to paint the walls of our brand-new house, just as my father demanded. I was on the second floor, pouring the remnants of the red container out in the main hallway, when I finally smelled smoke.

Stopping, I set the tank down on the ground, heading for the stairs, only to find the flames lazily climbing up each gasoline-covered step. There was no time to really *feel* the ice-cold flash of terror that rippled through me then. I had just poured fuel over every inch of the second floor, and if I didn't haul ass to somewhere safe, I would soon be swallowed up by the flames.

Thinking fast, I ran to the only room that wasn't covered in gas. My room. Just before the entire space erupted, I slammed my bedroom door shut, as if that thin piece of wood wasn't just as flammable as everything else in that house.

The smoke was creeping in from the crack of space left at the bottom, and the door immediately felt hot to the touch. In seconds the smoke in the room was thick and black like storm clouds prefacing the fiery hurricane that would soon destroy everything I owned.

I was coughing, unable to breathe until I rushed for the only window in the room, relieved to feel the winter chill on my face and fresh air in my lungs.

But it was a long way down.

It was the only way out, though.

I stared out unto the quiet suburban street, wondering when the firetrucks were coming. It was unlikely that they'd been called. The fire hadn't grown large enough for people to notice at almost four o'clock in the morning. I could yell for help, but that wouldn't change the fact that no one would be able to help me in time.

It was either jump or die.

My father's police cruiser was still in the driveway, as were the other cars, but there was no sign of him or my six-year-old brother out front. I tried to talk myself into it.

In the middle of my deliberation, a single body-chilling scream cut into the silence.

Desiree.

I knew it well. All of the blood in my body ran cold. You could almost forget that it was damn near two hundred degrees in that room. Of the hundreds of times I've heard my stepmother scream, sound had never ripped out of her quite like that. She was in pain. More pain than she'd ever been in. More pain than I think I've ever heard *anyone* be in.

Those flames were in her room before they got to mine. She was burning alive.

Alive.

I thought she had died. I thought that's why we were starting the fire in the first place, because Dad fucked up and broke her neck or something, and now we had to make it look like she died in a fire.

But she really *was* dying in a fire.

A fire that I helped feed.

I didn't even try to save her. To this day, I don't know if I would've been able to, but I would *never* know because too frozen in fear, I didn't even try.

My mother's screams ripped out of her as if her voice would try to escape the fire if her body could not. Whatever she was feeling—it was excruciating. And then it was so quiet. Even if the jump from the second story window broke every bone in my body, I knew such an outcome was no match for the agony of my mother's final moments.

So, that's what really pushed me to jump. It was selfish of me, but it seemed less terrifying to die from the impact of hitting the ground, than it would to burn alive. I deserved to be called a coward and all of its synonyms, but I found the courage to climb out onto the piece of slippery roof just below my sill and leap.

I landed on the lawn, wet with dew and cold, but I was grateful for it. When you've stared down the possibility of a fiery death, the thought of ever being cold again feels like a blessing.

It was a lucky fall. Of course, it hurt to hit the ground that hard and fast, but nothing on my body was broken. Landing on my back gave me a front row seat to watch as flames erupted out of my bedroom window, breaking the glass. Everything in my room was burning, and if I had waited even just a minute longer to jump, I would've been cooked.

The relieved smile on my face was short-lived, as the memory of my mother's agonized cries made its way back into my head. Like a never-ending echo trapped in the caves of my mind, replaying on a loop, reminding me of what I'd done.

Even if I couldn't say I killed her, I'd certainly played my part.

I don't know how long I laid in that wet grass, but for a second I feared I was the only person who made it out. I thought about my little brother, Sebastien, unsure if he was alive or dead. He was the only one of us who'd truly lost her. Unlike me, Sebastien really was half dad, half Desiree. *She* was his real mother and just as I was, Sebastien was terrified of our father. At six years old, our mother was all the nurturing parent he would ever have.

And now she was dead.

If Sebastien was dead, too, perhaps the blessing in that was that I wouldn't have to face him, having done what I did. I wouldn't have to tell a six-year-old boy that his mother was gone.

I got up from the ground, dusting off pieces of grass from my wet clothes. Shivering with that cold

January chill, my eyes were still glued on the burning house. I watched as fiery particles were picked up by the winter winds, and a thought crossed my mind.

Fire doesn't come from nowhere.

That forty-degree chill stuck to the moisture in my clothes as I walked around the collapsing house, toward the backyard. My thoughts should've been racing, but I was only thinking the same phrase over and over—*Fire doesn't come from nowhere.* Logic was beginning to outrun my emotional response, and it dawned on me that *somebody* had to have lit the first match.

It wasn't me.

"Dad?" I called out to him in the dead silence. It had to have been him, which meant he must've made it out. My lower back was a little sore from the impact with the ground, but I was walking just fine. "*Dad.*"

I heard Sebastien first. "Damien!"

My little brother was, of all things... *excited.* He popped into view, his yellowish complexion easy to find in the darkness. Sebastien was barely out of kindergarten; he didn't see the burning house behind us and fully understand how serious all of this was. He thought fire and explosions were cool and shit.

"Dame." Dad's voice emerged from the shadows, and maybe some small part of me had hoped he was dead, because I was disappointed to hear it. But at least I knew Sebastien was okay. My father walked out from the backyard's darkness and into a stream of light cast down from the burning house behind me. His voice sounded weird when he realized, "You made it out."

My father's tone was unmistakably... *dissatisfied*.

He tried to hide it, but it was clear that he wasn't happy to see that I was alright.

Taking note, I took a step back as one thing became obvious. I was fifteen years old the night my father murdered my mother. I didn't know it at the time, but he turned me into an accomplice. He set the fire, but I fertilized it with fuel. When it was all said and done, the house behind me had fallen to pieces by the time the sirens had arrived.

By then, I understood that my father had unsuccessfully tried to murder me, too.

The only unconditional love in this world is the love of money.

Money will make you do strange things.

Get a job you hate.

Move to a city you don't like.

Burn your house to the ground.

Try to kill your son.

Actually kill your wife.

Both of my parents had life insurance policies. One million dollars each. Whichever one of them died first would've made the other very rich. Talk about temptation. A million dollars might make even the most virtuous man think about... you know.

Unfortunately for my mother, Dad wasn't all that virtuous to begin with.

He wanted to make it look like a terrible accident.

I'm sure my father had it all planned out. His house caught fire; his wife and son didn't make it. That's the story that was supposed to be told. People would have a hard time believing a man murdered his wife by burning down his brand-new house. I mean, why buy the house at all, right? Even better, it might help that people wouldn't think the fire was started for life insurance money if a child died in the flames, too.

A discerning person might have the thought cross their mind and quickly chase it away. Because it is always a serious accusation to claim someone murdered their own wife. It is an even more serious—perhaps even disgusting—allegation to imply that someone might also murder their child. In the midst of such a tragedy, who was willing to be the person that would even *suggest* that the lives lost were premeditated? You'd have to be really cold, judgmental, and just one notch above paranoid, to speak those kinds of conspiracy theories out loud.

Except I didn't burn.

Unfortunately for my father, people don't have to conspiracy theorize when intended targets survive. There I was, standing in the dimly lit backyard without a scratch on me, an eyewitness to everything that had just transpired. My father's fate was to be sealed at the end of a detective's ballpoint pen, scribbling down my witness account. There was no way out of this.

Of course, he knew I wasn't going to lie for him. Not this time. Why would I? He tried to kill me.

When the firetruck sirens cut through that early morning stillness, I saw the panic in my father's face. I knew too much. I was a loose end. I think—for the briefest second—he thought about killing me with his bare hands.

I'm not a mind reader, so I'll never really know for sure, but I can vividly remember my father's wide-eyed stare in my direction. I can remember his slight squint as a thought crossed his mind. His hands twitched upwards as if he might reach for my neck, and then quickly went back down at the sounds of firemen calling out to survivors.

I'm not a mind reader, but I think the only reason my father didn't kill me in that moment was because he simply didn't have enough time to do it.

His shoulders fell, defeated.

I remember backing up a little, my eyes bouncing between him and my little brother. There was a lot going on in my mind. Still with the fresh memory of my mother's chilling screams as she burned, I grappled with the realization that my father tried to kill me tonight—not once, but twice.

This might sound pathetic, but as the shouting voices of the firemen grew closer, I actually *did* think about lying for him. When I was that age, I was desperate for my father's approval all the time. I might've actually considered lying for him if he'd even bothered to ask, but he didn't.

He just looked at me like I was holding a knife out to his chest, and he wasn't wondering if I would stab. He was just bracing himself for impact.

~

I was an accessory to murder.

Plain and simple. I had turned sixteen two days after the fire. Based off my honest confession, I was forced to share the blame for my mother's death. Sixteen was plenty old enough to know the difference between right and wrong. Sixteen is old enough to defy your father and recuse yourself from a murder plot. For that, the county prosecutor didn't see me as a victim at all.

This wasn't surprising. When have black boys ever been afforded the right to victimhood?

The case drew a lot of media attention. It was the kind of case that people sat around watching on their TVs. We were real people, but to the media, our story was one with villains and heroes and drama. Our lives became the kind of lives people would write books about, make movies out of, and reference for generations.

An esteemed black police officer woke up one morning and decided to murder his white wife so that he could add a couple more zeros on his bank balance. He enlisted the help of his awkwardly timid son, who wasn't related to her and therefore couldn't have loved her, and together they set their house on fire, burning his wife alive.

Who wouldn't pay to see that movie?

It's funny how anything can be demonized the moment people want to make you out to be a bad person. I was a quiet kid; always had been. Before my mother died, I was *just* a quiet kid.

After she died, the fact that I was quiet was suddenly suspicious. Maybe it meant I was a sociopath. Maybe it meant that I had sinister thoughts. Maybe it meant that I was hiding something evil just beneath the surface. In that time, I think there must've been hundreds of theories about me, with a million more people trying to figure me out.

Fortunately for me, at least *one* person in the growing audience around my life saw me for what I was.

A victim.

Fortunately for me, that one person was a lawyer, and she signed on to represent me in court. I was lucky. Martina Cross was a recent Stanford Law graduate, a thousand times better than anything the Broward County public defender's office would've given me.

She was young—younger than the average lawyer. Perhaps it was her youth that made her so optimistic about my impossible case. She wasn't jaded yet. She still believed in justice.

And she went to *Stanford*.

When prosecutors hear your legal counsel came out of a school like Stanford, they sweat a little. Cases that are supposed to be open-and-shut don't shut so easily anymore.

She was barely ten years older than I was, but I still called her Miss Martina. I think it reminded her that at the crux of it all, despite the fact that I was tall for my age, I was *just* a kid.

Most black boys past the age of thirteen are as good as grown men in the eyes of the system. They took in my sixteen-year-old face and saw no boyhood innocence. They couldn't imagine me fearing anything or anyone, because to them, I was the most fearsome thing in the room.

Simply put, Miss Martina wasn't part of the system—not yet at least. She saw me as something nobody else in that courtroom did—her little brother, a younger cousin, her future son. As far as she was concerned, I could've been any one of them.

And so, she fought for me like I was.

It was a long legal battle, one that would go on to expose the horrific physical and mental abuse I suffered at the hands of my father for fifteen years. The beatings, the neglect, the emotional turmoil.

The argument was that by the time the night of the fire rolled by, I was a broken person. My lawyer argued that I was not an accomplice, but a damaged child who'd been trained to do nothing but take orders.

All of this was true, but it was still difficult to argue. When viewers watch your life through a TV screen, it's easy for them to forget that you're a real person. To them, my mother was dead, and it was my fault just as much as it was my father's. Nobody cared that I cried almost every night because I missed her. Nobody cared that I loved her. Nobody cared that I blamed myself more than any of them ever could.

People are so inclined to see media figures as categorical—you're either good or you're bad. You're a person on a TV screen; you don't get to have depth

or flaws or feelings. You're either unrealistically perfect or you're guilty of everything they've ever accused you of. There is no in-between, no room for
nuance.

And I certainly wasn't... *good*.

So where did that leave me?

Innocent, I guess.

Kind of innocent.

That's what the juror who announced my verdict
said after he read it. Even though he wasn't required
to, he told the court that it was a very tough decision
to make and that four out of the twelve jurors who
sealed my fate still weren't sold on my innocence,
and they were *reluctantly* setting me free.

Miss Martina won me my freedom in the court of
law, but she couldn't help me in the court of public
opinion. My record was clean, but my world-famous
reputation was just too much.

For years, I would endure movie adaptations, true
crime documentaries, and books that painted me as
the murderer that got away. Black son, white mom; I
was like OJ Simpson, but *worse*... because the woman
I killed *raised* me.

I was innocent, but not really.

My father—however—he had no Miss Martina. If
my ordeal was bad, his was... unspeakable. Except,
he actually *earned* his problems. He hadn't even
been in the county jail for three months before he
turned up dead.

Nobody was surprised.

Former cops don't last long behind bars. Even less
if they've killed their wives.

Nobody mourned his death. There was no funeral. I got a tiny box of ashes in the mail with his first and last name scribbled on a sticker across the top in red Sharpie. It was a sobering realization—that enormous man that used to cast a chill deep into my bones, reduced to a box of dust no bigger than the palm of my hand.

For a while, I thought about opening that box and flushing his memory down the toilet. It would've been my only act of rebellion towards that man, because even as preparations were being made before he could stand trial, I never offered myself up to testify. I never even told anyone that he tried to kill me that night, too.

I just kinda kept it all in. A secret held between me and a box of ashes that I never got around to throwing away. Small as the box was, it always felt tremendously heavy; my father, Joseph Fine, an immortal nightmare that I carry with me always in a little brown box.

Through foster care, through young adulthood, through it all. Me and that little box.

A little over two years after my mother's death, I aged out of the system.

In just those two years, I'd moved through eight foster homes. It wasn't because I was a particularly difficult kid. I was just quiet. When you're both an accused killer *and* unusually quiet, it shouldn't surprise you that people don't want you around. My last seven months in the system were spent in a group home that felt quite like how I remembered jail.

I was thankful to turn eighteen and gain the option to leave.

Nine weeks after my eighteenth birthday, I was living in a South Florida homeless shelter on the day my life would change. I had my high school diploma, and I was going through the motions of enrolling at a community college nearby.

At that point, my life was aimless. I was an eighteen-year-old kid that couldn't walk into a McDonald's without getting whispered about. Every job I'd ever applied for had fallen through. Even fast-food joints refused to hire a matricidal monster that merely slipped through the cracks of a faulty legal system.

Even then, I knew that going to college was going to be a complete waste of my time.

But I was doing it anyway.

Even if nothing came out of getting a degree, it was something to do. And it was on the morning that I was meant to start my first day of classes that I was approached by a man in a suit.

He'd been looking for me for weeks following my eighteenth birthday. My enrolling in college made finding me all the more easy. This man had something to give me.

A check.

To the confused furrow of my brow, he explained that both my parents had life insurance policies. In the event that one of them died, the other was meant to receive one million dollars. In the event that *both* of them died, their children upon reaching legal adulthood, were to receive the payout. It didn't matter that one of them was murdered and the other one was killed in prison *for* murdering her. The insurance policies still stood.

That meant one million for me and one million for my younger brother when he was old enough. Like flicking a light switch, my financial situation changed overnight.

Just like that—a millionaire.

THE INTERVIEW

MORGAN

"Why do you want to attend Stanford Law School?"

Dr. Cross had been giving interviews all morning, talking for hours. That much was obvious from the looks of the white globs sticking at the corners of her mouth. It was hard not to stare at them as she spoke, watching the globs turn pink as they rubbed against her brick red lipstick. *Ew*, I thought, careful not to make a face, rising a thumb to the corner of my lips, wiping my own mouth just in case.

"Miss Caplan?" she said my name impatiently. I flinched, snatching my thumb away from my lips. Her eyebrows rose, waiting. *Did she ask me something just now?*

"I'm sorry." My back straightened out. *Shit. Shit. Shit.* "I'm sorry, Dr. Cross. Can you repeat the question?"

The inner corner of her right eyebrow pulled down, my only hint that she was irritated. Of course, she was irritated. She was only giving me the interview of a lifetime for my dream law school, and I... I was too preoccupied with the nasty, moist corners of her mouth.

Dr. Cross spoke more slowly this time, as if speaking to an idiot. "Why do you want to attend Stanford Law School?"

Because I'm trying to prove a point. Because once upon a time, my narcissistic ass daddy told me I was too stupid to ever amount to anything on my own, and the best that I could hope for was finding a man like him to take care of me till I die. 'It's a good thing you're pretty,' my father always used to say to me, but he would never mean it as a compliment.

Of course, I couldn't just say all of that in the middle of this interview. Dr. Cross was staring at me patiently waiting, and my eyes fell to the glass nameplate on her desk. Instead of thinking about my response, I wondered what the *A* in **Dr. Martina A. Cross** stood for.

Why isn't my brain working? I was frozen now, unable to recall the cookie-cutter answer I had rehearsed almost a hundred times before. *Why do I want to go to Stanford Law?* Something about helping people or giving back to my community or some other fake shit.

"Uh... um... Well..." My mind had gone blank. All I could see were judgmental brown eyes, staring a hole through me as I struggled to remember. All I could hear was the maddening *tock, tock, tock* of the clock overhead. *Is that clock hooked up to a speaker or something?* I broke eye contact with her, checking the time.

We had three minutes left in this interview.

My eyes snapped back down to Dr. Cross, and my breathing soon began to pick up when I realized something truly horrifying. I *couldn't* remember the question she'd just asked. Now, I was panicking. The law school interview is one foot in the door. Schools do not give out invitations to these things to people they don't want, so if you're lucky enough to get the interview, all you gotta do is *not* fuck it up, and you're in.

The first twenty-five minutes of my interview were amazing. I'd come into this room dressed in a powder pink power suit, head held high. My pixie cut black hair was laid perfectly to one side, my white manicure was shiny, and my focus was sharp. I was *ready.*

I was better than ready. I was confident.

I handled those first questions with ease—*light* work. But now, at the last question, I sat a stuttering dumbass, unable to remember something said ninety seconds before.

People don't always remember how you show up, but they *always* remember how you leave. And I was leaving this interview a failure.

"Relax." The irritation in Dr. Cross' eyes melted into pity. *You're pathetic,* I chastised myself. *She thinks you're pathetic.* "I was once intimidated when I was in that seat, too. Breathe."

I wasn't intimidated. I had a stupid brain fart.

Still, I took the opportunity to breathe myself down to a steady heartrate. She allowed me the time to self-compose. Dr. Cross was younger than I expected her to be, but then again, it could've been a trick of good genes. She was a pretty enough lady.

If I squinted my eyes and tilted my head to the side, she almost kinda looked like Kandi Burruss.

I knew from the two-tone paraphernalia on Dr. Cross' desk, that we were members of the same sorority, and my sorority was notorious for picking the pretty faces. Us having that in common helped me in the beginning of this interview, but even sorority sisterhood can't overlook unpreparedness.

Trying to regain my composure left me a lot of time to study her face.

Like me, she had a deep complexion and while she must've been at least twenty years my senior, the only sign of age on her skin were subtle wrinkles at the corners of her mouth. A pristine face with laugh lines, a sign that she was the type to smile big and often.

Behind me, there was a quick knock at the office door, breaking the silence before I could attempt to answer her question again.

A woman with her eyes on an iPad came stepping into Dr. Cross' office. Without looking up from the tablet, she announced, "Damien is on the phone for you, Tina."

Dr. Cross cleared her throat. "Bailey."

The woman looked up from the iPad and her brown eyes widened, seemingly surprised that I was still in here. They stared at each other, communicating in complete silence with subtle facial expressions. Bailey—a personal assistant, I assumed—confusedly checked the silver smartwatch on her wrist.

I checked the clock behind Dr. Cross' head, noting that I had run six minutes over time.

"We're running a little late. Please tell Damien I'm in a meeting."

"You want me to tell *Damien Fine* to wait? How long?" Bailey asked, something panicked about her tone, emphasizing the man's name like there was something important about it. I recognized it vaguely, like I might've heard of him once while watching the news or something. Evidently, he must've been important if Bailey was stunned at how I wasn't immediately kicked out of the office at the mention of his name.

Dr. Cross seemed to consider this as well, picking up the phone on her desk. "Forward the call."

As Bailey's heels clicked out of the office, Dr. Cross turned her attention back to me, snapped repeatedly, and rushed, "Quickly. Why Stanford Law School?"

I blinked several times and then tried to rush my response, "Because I've wanted to come here since I was a little girl and—"

"That's enough. Good," she stopped me when the light on her office phone flashed green. Bringing the receiver to her ear, she held it up with her shoulder and searched her desk for something to write with. "Hello, Damien. No—I wasn't in the middle of anything. Sorry for the wait. My assistant is hopeless."

Dr. Cross spoke as if I was no longer sitting in front of her, eventually finding a pen and scribbling a note on a yellow Post-It. She slid it over to me as she laughed at something the man on the other end of the phone must've said.

I reached for the note, hoping it would say something encouraging.

Have Bailey validate your parking. Enjoy the rest of your Friday.

My expression fell.

Conscious of the fact that she seemed to be on an important call, I tried to be as quiet as possible as I started to leave, whispering a polite, "Thank you."

She put a finger to her maroon lips immediately, ordering me silent. In her eyes, the pity from before melted back into irritation. *Fuck*, I thought.

A little embarrassed, I quickly tried to step out of the office, cringing with each step I took because my heels made it impossible to walk silently. I closed Dr. Cross' office door slowly as I stepped back into the main reception lobby.

There, Bailey sat at her desk, clicking away at the computer in front of her. I stopped at her corner, pulling out my parking stub from the back pocket of my dress pants. Bailey's desk, like Dr. Cross', was adorned with the same signature colors of my sorority. A little part of me hoped this meant that Dr. Cross was the type to give fellow sorors opportunities. Maybe there was hope for me yet.

I didn't say a word as I slid my stub across the desk. Bailey grabbed the parking receipt and calculated the cost in her head before printing out my credit.

"You look like you're about to be sick," she commented as we waited for it to print. She looked to be around my age, which might've made me get too comfortable, because I immediately started unloading my fears on her.

"I don't think I could've been any worse in there," I told her. "I messed it up so bad."

Bailey nodded politely, but I could tell she didn't care. Dozens of law school hopefuls must've passed through this office every week, looking just as defeated as I likely did now. Still, she tried to reassure me, "Listen, Martina's on a phone call with a billionaire who is poised to donate several millions of dollars to the school. Whatever you did in that room—I promise you she's not thinking about it right now, sweetie."

She handed me my parking credit.

"I wouldn't stress. If she nabs the donation—knowing her, you just might get in off the good mood that puts her in." Bailey ran her manicured fingers through her wavy black bob before adding, "I'm really good at guessing which of the interviewees have a shot at getting in. I've got a good feeling about you. If Dr. Cross didn't like you, she wouldn't have given you extra time like that. You didn't hear it from me, but I think you can relax."

THE DOMINATRIX

DAMIEN

"I don't like quiet guys like you. I always feel like they're judging me."

"You've got low self-esteem, Tee." I was shouting over the mid-volume *oontz-oontz* music that these hipster San Franciscans love so fuckin' much.

"See? There it is." Martina licked a glob of salt off her little brown wrist, tossing back a shot of tequila before squeezing a lime into her mouth. We were in the heart of downtown San Francisco, tucked away in some backroom booth in this rundown shack she was calling a speakeasy. All the lights in here were red LEDs, turning Martina's brown eyes burgundy as she shot both her middle fingers up at me. "You so fuckin' judgey, you know that? Why the face anyway? This bar too ghetto for you, rich boy?"

There was that Miami girl twang of hers, which was always strongest when she was drunk and having fun. It was nothing like the fancy pants law professor chick she played during the day. Sometimes I'd forget that she could sound like this—her prissy NorCal accent would always flow out of her like she was born and raised in the Bay. But Martina could codeswitch like second nature, and when we were together, we would always fall back to those kids from Florida we used to be.

"You got something to say about my face every time I see you. This is just how I look, Tee."

"What a pity." She tossed her head back as she said it. "You'd be so handsome if you wasn't so ugly."

We didn't grow up together or anything; it just kind of felt like we did since we were from the same place. We both spoke the same language. In all actuality, Martina was already twenty-six by the time she met me in a South Florida jail visitation room. Already a freshman lawyer by then, she looked at my sixteen-year-old face and told me then, *'You don't belong here, and I'm gonna get you out, kid.'*

I *did* belong there.

But she did get me out.

We'd been friends ever since, and when I was old enough for that ten-year gap in our ages to not feel so strange, we became *best* friends. So much so that when she called me a few days ago, asking if I might be willing to throw her school a few dollars in her honor, I wrote a check with eight zeros.

Martina, as far as I could remember, had only ever asked me for help twice.

The first time was when I asked her what she wanted for Christmas nine years ago. She had jokingly told me to pay off her six-figure student loan debt. I wasn't even a billionaire back then, but I didn't even hesitate to pay off the entire balance. The second time was five years ago, after her ex-wife got to keep the house in the divorce. She said rent in the Bay Area was like highway robbery, so I told her to pick out a house and I'd get it for her.

I would always have her back. She had mine when she stood to gain nothing from it, and I would never forget that. For how she saved my life, I should owe Martina a lifetime of favors. And yet despite my ever-growing net worth, she still didn't make a habit out of asking me for things. So, when she finally got around to needing my help again, I made sure she *really* knew how much I appreciated her this time.

Tonight, we were celebrating. Not just because it was my birthday, but because I'd given her the number earlier this morning.

"Oh *my God*, Damien." Martina slipped back into her grating NorCal cadence to gush. Her voice was louder than the house music that shook the shabby red furniture underneath us. "You should've *seen* their faces when I told them how much you were giving to the school. At first they kinda turned their noses up at the thought of taking your money." She squinted sympathetically. "You know how it is." *Of course, I know.* "But even they could never scoff at *nine* fucking figures, Damien. Shit—are your finances gonna be straight with you giving away that much money?"

"Yeah." I nodded, trying to finish up the last of the bourbon in my glass. *You're such a southern boy,*

Martina would always say every time I ordered it. "My finances are gonna be just fine."

"Ugh, if I wasn't so gay, I'd suck your dick—I *swear* I would." Martina just shook her head while I choked on my drink, the howl rumbling up from my chest shot a splatter of bourbon onto the table. "I'm dead serious, too."

"I believe you," I told her, still smiling as the last of my laughing subsided. I ordered a third round of drinks for the table, tequila, lime, and salt for her, another bourbon for me. "Who you gonna name the scholarship after?"

"*You*, of course!" She swatted my shoulder for even asking, that pin straight black hair of hers brushing against my arm before she pulled back. "I wanna call the recipients Fine Scholars. And I don't care what the school has to say about it either, Damien. You were found innocent in a court of law, and if anybody needs to respect that, it's a fuckin' law school, you hear me?"

Even at my now grown age of thirty-three, Martina never got out of the habit of talking to me like I was her little brother getting bullied at school. To her, I was always gonna be that sixteen-year-old kid that used to get jumped in the prison yard, showing up with new cuts and bruises on his face every time she came to update him on his case. It was like she couldn't even see that I got older; that I got stronger. I wasn't that kid anymore. I hadn't been for a really long time.

Her doting ways used to annoy me when I was in my twenties. Back then I was trying so fucking hard to forget I was ever that soft. But now I understood that that's just how Martina was, and it was no use arguing with her over the way she showed love.

"Fine Scholars." It would join the long list of other scholarships and buildings around the country that were named after me on account of my money. "I like that."

"I *love* it," Martina's drunk ass chimed in. "And best of all—thanks to *you*, Mr. Fine—I'm getting *alllllllll* the credit. Biggest donation in the history of Stanford University, and who got it for 'em? Me—Dr. Martina Aubrielle Cross. And so, you know who they better make Dean of Admissions & Financial Aid when Dean Warhol's ole rickety ass gets ready to retire?"

I felt my cheek lift with a smile. She'd been talking about wanting that position since she started working at her alma mater ten years ago. "You'll get it."

"I better get it, because it took me *six... long... ye ars...* to even get on the admissions committee and I don't think I have it in me to keep doing all this admissions grunt work." She licked another dab of salt off the back of her hand, downed her tequila, and munched on a lime wedge before whining, "I'm *not* cut out for this interviewing law school hopefuls shit."

"Let me hear it," I invited her to vent. This was the thoughtful side of me that only she ever got to see. Martina was a relic of my past. No matter how rich or powerful I'd become, she knew the timid, softspoken Damien first. Our history gave me a kind of comfort to not always have to be so hard when it was just me and her. Ever since my father burned it down, Martina was as close to a home as I ever had.

"Take today, for instance." Martina was talking over her empty third glass. "I'm interviewing this girl this morning. Gorgeous girl, really. I saw so much of myself in her at first. Very strong application. High GPA, high test scores. Decent interview. She's from Miami, like me. She even pledged my sorority."

I heard the inevitable 'but' coming. "But..."

"*But!*" she emphasized, getting a little loud. "Here I am, fully prepared to push her application through, welcome this bitch to Stanford and whatnot... and *then*..." Martina shook her head, looking like she might be sick. She cleared her throat, and lowered her voice, "We run all our applicants through this advanced web sweep. It's supposed to catch things like racist social media posts, criminal convictions, et cetera. But *this* girl..."

I waited for her to finish.

Martina shook her head again, making her shiny black hair sway from side to side. "I can show you better than I can tell you. Pull out your phone." So, I did. "Type into Google, '*Mistress Morgan*' with no spaces." She waited until she was sure that the site was loaded on my screen and then exclaimed, "*Look* at what I almost let in."

On my phone was a sleek red and white webpage. *Mistress Morgan* was scrawled across the top in black cursive, and underneath was a photo of a girl. She had deep brown skin, barely covered by the black lace lingerie she had on. Her hair was cut to one of those very short boyish styles, but she pulled it off femininely since her face was very pretty. In her hands, she balanced a long black whip on one knee, poised atop thigh-high black boots. The look on her face was fearsome—or at least, her best attempt at it. She wasn't as intimidating as she obviously wanted to come off. If I had seen her out in public somewhere, I might've thought she was adorable, nowhere near close to scary.

There was a short message written under the single photo:

Sometimes you just need a woman's touch...
But there's nothing gentle about mine.
Are you ready to be punished?
Prideful men need not apply.

"So, she's a dominatrix," I realized, more amused than shocked, scrolling down the site as more sexy photos of her came in full view.

It was one particular picture of her that made my sliding finger freeze. A closer shot of her face—the kind of picture people always take when they know they look good. Like in all the other photo, she was doing her very best to seem intimidating, the pierce of her big, brown-eyed gaze exaggerated so much that I chuckled. Again, I just thought she was cute. It made me wonder how anyone could pay her to dominate them, with her looking like a little girl trying on grown women's shoes. Mistress Morgan didn't look a day over twenty-two, if I were to guess.

Noting the growing smirk on my face, Martina cleared her throat loudly, extra obnoxious with it. I pressed the power button on my phone, stuffing it back in my pocket to meet her eyes.

With a shrug, I said, "She's cute. What is she, twenty-two?"

"Twenty-three," Martina corrected through gritted teeth and barely moving lips. "It's bad enough that I'm forced to interview all these bright-eyed, empty-headed twenty-somethings, all pretending to give a shit about impacting society and helping the less fortunate... but now the committee is also sending me pretty little prostitutes." Martina held her face between her hands. "I'm so *over* this fucking job."

I squinted, understanding what Martina was saying without saying. "So, you're not gonna let her in?"

"There you go with that judgey ass face again." Martina smiled wryly at the question. "Don't think with your dick, Damien. Think with that big brain of yours. For every law school acceptance I push through, my name goes down with it." The NorCal snob was thick in her voice now. Martina from Miami doesn't talk like this, but Martina from San Francisco talks like this all the time. "Stanford is a very prestigious institution—a top three law school. If I let her in, and any of those clickbait news sites find her booking page as easily as we just did, think of the headlines. *'You Won't Believe How THIS Stanford Law Student Pays Her Tuition'.* That's a viral news story if I've ever heard one, and I refuse to put my name anywhere near that inevitable media circus."

"You're telling me she's a hundred percent qualified, but you're gonna ax her application because of how she makes her money." That bothered me a lot. *Why does this bother me so much?* From the confused scrunch of Martina's brows, I could tell she was asking herself the same question. "And you think I'm the judgey one?"

"Are we fighting right now? Over this shit? It feels like we're fighting. There's no way you even really *care*," Martina rebuffed. "You just think she's pretty."

"I *do* think she's pretty." I could admit that. Why did finding her pretty make my point any less valid? "But I'm not wrong. You said yourself that she's qualified."

"She's also *selling pussy* on Bill Gates' internet, Dame." Both her hands were up like she was urging me to challenge her point.

My point was better. "If she wanted to do that for the rest of her life, I doubt she'd be trying to get into law school."

Martina then rolled her eyes extra slow.

"I need you to say that last part again. Because you're *absolutely* right—it's a law school." Something about this conversation was sobering Martina up in spite of her three shots of tequila. This wasn't harmless banter. We were actually arguing. "Stanford is not a fuckin' keep-you-off-the-streets after school program. I don't give a damn if you think it's unfair. It's my call to make. And I should've never told your benevolent ass about it anyway. You think you gotta be a saint just 'cause everybody in the world thinks you killed your stepmother and got away with it, but that self-righteous schtick gets annoying sometimes, you know."

I hate getting into arguments with lawyers. They don't know how to admit it when they're wrong. And they always take it too far. We just kind of stared at each other, both of us in brand-new bad moods as the *annoying* ass house music played in the background. Martina's glaring eyes glowed burgundy under the overhead red lights, but her expression was the first to soften.

"Now you're getting quiet on me. I hate it when you get quiet on me, *Damien*. It always makes me feel like you're—"

"I am."

My Sanctuary

Morgan

"I don't wanna go to a school that names scholarships after murderers anyway."

Lauren stopped holding her breath and uncrossed her fingers. The dimples in her cheeks disappeared. My twin sister's face was identical to mine, so the way I watched her features turn sad matched *exactly* what I felt inside.

"You didn't get in?" Her disappointed voice vibrated from my iPhone speakers, filling my Miami condo. This was not the celebratory FaceTime call she thought we were gonna have. In my hand, her face was soft with sympathy, *'are you gonna be okay?'* practically oozing from her big brown eyes.

Why would they do this? Everything about my application—my GPA, my test scores, my internships—were perfect.

"Just last week, I read on Twitter that Stanford *actually* took, like, two hundred million dollars from that dude who killed his stepmother up in Fort Lauderdale when we were kids. I'm good, Lauren. I don't wanna go to a school like that anyhow." I made light of the situation even though what I really wanted to do was go out onto my balcony and scream at the night sky until my throat was bloody.

I'm going to apply again, next cycle. Of course, I didn't tell my sister that right away because I couldn't both downplay the sting of rejection and announce that I was going to try again.

As sympathetic as she was, my sister couldn't relate. Lauren was far away in New England, living with the love of her life, well on her way to being a doctor and becoming the grand success our father always said she would be.

When we were kids, daddy used to make my twin and me compete. The asshole didn't have it in him to love two kids at the same time, so whichever one of us got the highest grades, won the most awards, and made the most sports teams—that's the one he cared about.

Because of him, I used to *hate* Lauren when we were little girls.

In our daddy's eyes, I was supposed to. You don't make nice with the people you're trying to step on, even if it's family.

It's sad, really. Because Lauren was supposed to have been my best friend all along. God gave us to each other the day we were born, and just like the devil, daddy swooped in, and derailed what the Lord intended.

But Lauren and I couldn't stay enemies for long. You can never really hate your twin—it's like hating yourself. We got older and we left him and his toxic bullshit behind. We even left mama, too, because she didn't wanna leave him and come with us.

For a while now, Lauren and I have been our own little family, and we were doing just fine.

"You're my best friend, you know that?" I asked the cell phone screen.

"Oh *noooo*," Lauren whined, pushing thick twist-out strands away from her eyes. "You always talk like this when you're trying not to cry. There are other law schools, Mor. You applied to other schools, right?"

I only applied to one. For me, it was Stanford or bust, my first and only choice. I had a point to prove.

Our father, in his heyday, was a bigshot Florida state prosecutor. Just like Lauren, daddy never had a problem rising through the ranks of any syndicate he waltzed into. He was an ambitious go-getter; it's part of what made him such a malignant narcissist, part of why he used to bully me so bad.

Daddy spent so much of my life reminding me that I was the least impressive member of our family.

'It's a good thing you're pretty,' daddy would always say to me, but even that wasn't unique because my perfect sister Lauren looked *just* like me. There was no room for unremarkable in daddy's world, and so in turn, there was never any room for me.

Even if he never found out about it, it had always been my dream to just do the one thing he *couldn't* do.

"Daddy got rejected from Stanford Law, too, you know. Back in the eighties."

"I know. He used to bitch about it all the time back in the day," Lauren replied, rolling her eyes and shrugging.

"That's why I gotta go." I wasn't doing it for him; I was doing it for me. Because it would make me feel good. "It's the only place I applied to."

My sister frowned one of those cartoonish, lips all the way turned down, frowns.

Her eyes through the screen were compassionate, and she let out a big sigh. I knew what that look meant; that was that '*daddy broke your spirit and you're still trying to fix it*' look. Sometimes Lauren and I could talk to each other with just facial expressions and long exhales. Twin language, she'd call it. '*I really wish I could help you,*' her eyes said to me now. '*I wish you could help me, too,*' my eyes said back.

I felt like crying so fucking bad.

Lauren was on the verge of tears herself when she whined, "What am I going to *do* with you?" I gave her a sad smile, feeling the *only* tear I would shed over this rejection letter slide down my cheek. "You gotta let him go like I did, Mor."

Daddy might've favored Lauren, but that didn't mean he loved her either. He had such high expectations of her, that he damn near killed her trying to make her perfect. That's why we left together, because it was good for both of us.

"It's easier for you than me. He doesn't live in your head like he lives in mine." I brought up a hand to wipe my face before announcing my next course of action. "I'm gonna add some more lines to my résumé and apply again next year."

"You don't have to go to a stupid school to be worth a damn, Morgan."

Yes, I do.

"I know that, Lauren, but I've been wanting this ever since I was five years old. You know this." I forced a smile, knowing my dimples were showing now. "Tell me I can do it."

"*Of course*, you can," she said without hesitation, her eyes darting to something off screen, and I could hear the sound of a door shutting on her side. "Kain just got home. Do you wanna say hi?"

I shook my head, not in the mood to talk to Lauren's Ivy League fiancé, while trying to process my own failures. *Everybody seems to be doing big things but you. When will it be your turn, Morgan?* "Just tell Kain hi for me. I gotta get to work now anyway."

"Everything is going to be *okay*." With a beaming smile, Lauren tried to get those last few words of encouragement in, her doe eyes twinkling, hoping her forced upbeat energy might rub off on me. Just before I ended the video call, she reminded, "Chin up, twin. I hate to see my face looking so sad."

~

"Did I say you could cum?"

The two of us were alone again, nestled in the privacy of my downtown work studio.

The pale man below me was on all fours atop my crimson bedspread, six pink stripes on his naked ass growing more red by the second. At least three days a week, Ian Lieberman would always make time to stop by the studio. It was the only place he felt safe enough to really be him. Here, without judgement, he could live out his submissive fantasies.

Here, we could both be different people.

I was harsher the second time I hissed, "Who *the fuck* said you could cum?"

Ian's voice was a frightened whisper, dripping with shame. "I'm sorry, Mistress."

These little games were therapeutic for me as well. Power is addictive, and when I was in the studio, I got to have as much of it as I wanted. This was my safe space, too.

People in my life thought I made all my money selling hair on the internet, and while I did have a little online business where I sold Malaysian bundles and wigs, neither my friends nor my sister knew about the website that *really* paid my bills.

Outside of this room, I was pre-law Morgan Caplan.

But when I was here, I was badass Mistress Morgan.

The studio was a small efficiency apartment that I owned and operated on the outskirts of downtown Miami. Here, there were no windows, and the walls were painted black on all sides except for one which was bloody red. In the center of the small unit was a king size bed with a red satin bed set, and in every other corner, I had my tools—canes, whips, chains, cuffs, ball gags, the whole arsenal. All sorts of men would come in and out of this apartment, each with a different preference for what they wanted done to them, but the one thing that remained consistent was me.

I was the one in charge here.

"I didn't mean to cum, Mistress."

"And yet..." I blinked several times, my grip on the black cane tightening. I was supposed to have given him ten lashes, but by the time I got to the sixth, he came too fast. "...look at what you freaking did to my sheets, Ian! What part of *'you only get to cum when I tell you, you can,'* don't you understand?"

"I am very sorry, Mistress. I'll buy you new sheets, Mistress. A new mattress, Mistress. Whatever you need, Miss—"

"Stop talking." A deep crease formed between my brows. The Stanford rejection from earlier had put me in a bad mood, and I might've been hitting Ian much harder than I usually would. It obviously got him too excited. See, Ian was one of those clients that got off on me being especially mean to him. "I don't even want to finish this session anymore. You don't deserve the rest of my time tonight."

Really, I just wanted to be alone and still get paid for it. If I could mask this shortened session as a punishment for something he'd done wrong, I'd still get my money in full.

My trembling submissive was slowly getting up, obvious pain on his face because the growing welts on his behind must've been a little sore. Without my asking, the naked man was removing the red fitted sheet from my mattress. He was the only one of us who was nude. Usually, when I was servicing clients, I did so in a shiny faux leather bodysuit.

Clothes set the silent hierarchies of my studio.

I don't get naked for men who submit to me.

It reminds the submissives, who come in and out of this apartment, of their place.

"I can still stay and clean up after myself."

"Ian, I don't know who the fuck you think you're talking to."

"I'm so sorry, Mistress," he said quickly, immediately trying to walk back that fatal misstep. All my subs needed to end every sentence with *Mistress* when they addressed me. It's a sign of respect. "I meant to say, I can stay behind and clean up after myself, *Mistress.*"

"*Of course* you will." I was quietly stepping around him, removing the black lace gloves that went up to my elbows. Frantically, Ian ran around the bed, collecting sheets and pillowcases into jittery hands. From a black leather couch on the far end of the room, I was seated as I watched while he carefully fluffed my pillows before neatly placing the soiled linens into a laundry pile.

With hands full, he stopped when I stuck out a leg to block him from going any further. He kept his head down, just like I told him he should when we started these weekly sessions two and a half years ago. With eyes to the ground, Ian made sure there wasn't any masculine timbre in his voice when he asked, "May I please walk past, Mistress?"

I didn't move. "Why are you still naked?"

"You haven't given me permission to put my clothes on, Mistress."

My voice was extra icy when I asked, "Do you think I want your *nasty* little dick dripping cum all throughout my studio then?"

"I don't think you do, Mistress."

"Then why don't you cover that thing up," I suggested, knowing full well that I would've had something to say if he had gotten dressed without my permission anyway. Between us, there were no right answers. Ian walked on a very fine line, knowing deep down that I'd always find something to snap at him for.

And that's why he paid me at a premium, because my particular brand of mean did it for him every time. Even now, I could see his flaccid penis beginning to harden as he rushed to put his clothes back on. Ian liked to be mercilessly put in his place. The more awfully I treated him, the more aroused he became, and the more eager he was to please.

"Look me in the eyes," I instructed. Clients are only allowed to look at me when I've given them the permission. His head rose so that his green eyes could meet mine, body nervous and periodically bouncing from side to side before finally relaxing. He was a timid sort of guy, pale white skin dotted with just about a thousand brown freckles. The man was in his early forties with thin red wisps of hair covering his balding head.

He was what I liked to call a *'normie'*, because when he wasn't here, he likely seemed extremely vanilla. I knew he was a divorced father with two young sons in elementary school. Outside of these walls, he was kind of a big shot commercial architect with the respect of his peers. Surely, no one would suspect that he liked to spend his Monday, Wednesday, and Friday evenings with a twenty-three-year-old dominatrix who he paid very well to treat him like shit.

When we first met, he was married. I'm not proud of that, but I was a sex worker. If I turned my services off to married men, I would never get any business. Ian told me once that he would lie awake at night, wondering if his wife would respect him less if she knew what he was really into.

I would think about Ian's poor unsuspecting wife, too. Maybe one time he might've asked her to slap him in bed and she didn't do it hard enough. Maybe he once asked her to call his dick little and gross and she, thinking that couldn't possibly be what he wanted to hear, told him that it wasn't. He loved her so much, but she would never understand him.

The woman had no idea who she married.

She had my pity right up until the day she divorced him. *Good for her*, I thought when I found out. I'm always happy to see wives leave their husbands. It's very rare I meet a man who *actually* deserves his woman. Plus, it was good for business now that Ian had so much more free time.

Ian Lieberman was one of my longest-running clients. He was actually one of my very first clients. Over the last two years, men would come and go, but never Ian. Three times a week from six to nine PM, he was at my apartment door, desperate to be dominated.

Ian was the best kind of submissive; never gave me any lip, generous with his money, and he had a high pain tolerance. He wasn't allowed to fuck me—none of my clients were—but out of all of them, he seemed to be the most okay with that. I would never tell him this, but he was actually my favorite.

From the couch, I served a final order.

"After you put those sheets in the washing machine, you can leave my money on the dryer before you go." This was the only place in the world where I could ever have this much audacity, my happy place.

My sanctuary.

Ian's balding little head nodded obediently. "Of course, Mistress."

Damien

Sebastien was waiting for me in the hallway when I got home.

My apartment was at the top of an eighty-story building in Downtown Miami's financial district. They call this part of the city Wall Street South. The newspapers will tell you that it's because South Florida is quickly becoming a bustling financial hub, but really it's because I live here now.

Sebastien always comes by when he needs money.

"It's just five G's this time," he reasoned nonchalantly, as though he were asking for a twenty.

When I arrived home from the airport that morning, my brother had been leaning against the door frame of my apartment's threshold. Sebastien could be real disrespectful when he got needy. Even now, he wasn't even *asking* me for money—he was just *telling* me how much he expected to be given, as if my agreement was already guaranteed.

Not many people can step to me the way I let Sebastien get away with.

Perhaps it's because, like Martina, I felt like I owed my little brother something. I felt as though I might owe him for the rest of my life. And of that he was perfectly aware. Because whether I meant to or not, I took something from Sebastien that I'll never be able to give back.

I didn't say anything to him as I unlocked the front entryway, quietly walking into my dark apartment and leaving the door slightly opened behind me. I could hear Sebastien slipping past the threshold from behind, equally silent as I set my keys down in the foyer.

He shut the door.

A little less than an hour from where I grew up, my apartment was like an estate in the sky. Floor to ceiling windows wrapped around the entire space, right in the middle of the busy Miami metropolis, offering picturesque snapshots of the city and a panoramic view of Biscayne Bay. Even smack dab in the center of everything, it was quiet up here.

Sebastien flipped a switch, lighting the living room and making small talk. "You didn't tell me you were going out of town for so long. Where did you go?"

My brother looks just like me.

At twenty-three, Sebastien was ten years younger, and it should've been easy to tell, but even considering the age difference it was by complexion that most people told us apart. I'm dark like dad and he's light like Desiree, while everything else about our faces is the same. It's possible that I just looked good for my age, but I used to joke that it was his white side making him look older than he should.

Or it might've been all the drugs he was on.

Sebastien would try very hard to obscure the resemblance. And I can't exactly say that I blame him on account of the fact that he shared a face with the likes of somebody as infamous as me. It's why, in the last two years, he grew his brown hair out into chin-length dreads and covered every bit of his exposed skin in ink.

The tattoos would make it hard to see his track marks, but I could always tell when he'd been using from the way his hazel eyes would dilate so much that his irises looked black.

He's high right now, I quietly determined under the light of my kitchen.

"You was in California again?" Sebastien asked, answering his own question from before. "I saw on the news that you gave Martina's school, like, two hundred mill." He whistled, shaking his head. "All that for her? If I didn't know any better, I would think you and that dyke was fuckin'."

Sometimes you just gotta let the dope fiends in your life talk. You don't even really have to say anything in response. They like the sounds of their own voices.

I set my carry-on on the ground beside the black stone island in the kitchen, starting up the espresso machine to make myself something strong. After being out west for more than a month, my mind was still running on California time. Even though it was eight o'clock in the morning and the sun was high in the sky, my brain was convinced it was five.

"Did you eat breakfast yet?" *That cocktail of shit he's on makes him so fuckin' skinny.*

"Nah, I ain't here for no food." Sebastian shook his dreads tiredly, backing out of the kitchen toward the living room. We had a complicated relationship, my baby brother and I, but on our good days, we might actually be friends. "Can I have some money, Dame?"

He probably doesn't remember him much, but Sebastien sounds just like our dad. Especially when he calls me that.

"I don't think you can today, Bash." Of course, his neutral expression disappeared, and with it went his cordiality, I'm sure. That paper thin mask of his disintegrated when he stepped back into my personal space, and I instantly knew we wouldn't be friends today. Nonchalantly, I asked, "Could you at least wait until I finish my coffee before you start cussin' me out?"

"*Fuck you*, Damien!"

"Guess not."

"Nah, nah, nah, nah, nah." He got louder with each progressive '*nah*', pacing through the kitchen as he ran his fingers through his locs. "'Cause I wanna know why you got all this fuckin' money for charities and universities and everybody else who ain't me, but soon as I ask you to throw something my way, you wanna act cheap."

You'd think I'd never given the kid money a day in his life.

The more self-aware corners of my mind understood that I played a significant role in making Sebastien the way he was. None of this happened overnight.

After I was arrested at sixteen, Sebastien was only six and orphaned.

They sent him to go live with Desiree's people, and even when I was able, I didn't try to get him out of there. He was with them for nine long years. It's precisely because he never talks about his time there that I know they must've given him hell. And why wouldn't they? He was her parents' little mixed reminder—half their blue-eyed angel, and half the nigga that killed her.

Sebastien never had to tell me that those people didn't love him. It was obvious to me. 'Cause my brother ran away at fifteen, and I knew for a fact they didn't look for him.

But I did.

By then, I was twenty-five, living in New York, but for him, I moved back to Florida. In those days,

Sebastien really knew how to take advantage of my guilt. I'd say no to some dumbass shit like a sportscar he didn't even know how to drive, and then all of a sudden, he was crying about how much he missed Desiree. And just like that, he'd get the sportscar, or whatever else he wanted that week. He was so fuckin' manipulative. Even when I wanted to, it was just so hard to say no.

It took me too long to realize that Sebastien couldn't even remember Desiree anymore.

Shit, I probably missed her more than he did.

By the time I stopped indulging him, he was already too damn spoiled. I still remember how he trashed my old apartment when I took his credit card away. It was the first time I ever had to physically fight my little brother. That day I broke two of his ribs and busted his lip. And the bruises... He was so damn light skinned, that *for weeks,* the purples and blues on his skin reminded me of what I did.

That's the only time he's ever looked like Desiree to me.

I promised myself I'd never do that to him again, but unfortunately I would. Several times. He was just so good at pushing my buttons, so good at turning me into our dad.

When my brother turned eighteen, he finally got his half of the life insurance money. By then, we were two enemies living in the same house, and so he left without even telling me. I didn't hear from him for six months after that. Honestly, it was the most peaceful six months I'd had in a minute at that point. For that, I didn't look for him. And I regret that decision every day. 'Cause when he came back broke and homeless, I was confused for a minute about how he managed to blow through a million dollars in six months, but it all made sense when I realized the kid was now addicted to like a dozen different drugs.

Of course, I tried to put him in rehab, but you can't fix people who don't think that they're broken. The best I could do for him was put him up in an apartment nearby, and make sure someone gets his groceries because I know he'd always forget to.

These days, I was perfectly aware of the fact that Sebastien was using my money to feed his habits. But I also knew that if I stopped giving him cash, he'd just look for cheaper alternatives; fuck around and shoot up something laced that could kill him. At least if I gave him money, I knew he'd be using the good stuff. The safer stuff.

All I asked was that he never show up to my fuckin' house high. *That's it.*

I guess I just didn't like to see where my money was going.

"What's five thousand dollars to you anyway, huh?" Sebastien was having one of those dope fiend tantrums while I poured a steady stream of black espresso into a mug. "That's nothing to you. You could wipe your ass with five G's."

"You know what?" I drank a bit of the americano and looked at him. "I think I might."

If looks could kill, he would've killed me with the way his eyes turned to slits when he glared. The anger was murderous, and I'm sure that if he didn't know I could easily have him on his ass, he would've tried something. Sebastien was an addict, not stupid.

He tried to appeal to my sympathies instead. "Why you always judging me?"

"I'm not judging you, kid."

"Yes, you are." Sebastien shook his head, choosing to look at my shirt instead of my eyes. I finished up the last of my coffee. "You're so hung up on that petty shit—what people think. Your reputation. You think that if you give away enough money, you might start to be known for it. That's how you want people to see you—Mr. Big Shot Billionaire Philanthropist." His eyes darkened then. "You want them to forget about how you killed my mom?"

Here we go.

"I'm not doing this—"

"You can't *judge* me! You can never fuckin' judge me! You *owe* me! You owe me *for life*!" He was shouting, and if I didn't own the entire top floor, there might've been neighbors around to hear him do it. "All those people you tryna impress—you don't owe them *shit*! It's me, Dame! It's me you gotta answer to!"

"*What the fuck* did I tell you, huh?" I finally set the mug in my hands down, getting in his face. I never set out to hurt him, but he knew I'd lay hands on him if pushed. It's likely that Sebastien can't remember him, but I'm sure that somewhere in his subconscious, he knows I sound just like dad when I get like this. It's obvious in the way that he shrinks at the first sign of it. I hate to see it, but it's only when I'm like this that he listens. "You're not fooling anybody right now. I can see it in your fuckin' eyes! If you can't stay straight long enough to make it to my house and beg, before you go off and catch your next hit then I'm not giving you *shit*. I told you already."

He backed out of my face, taking some of that bass out his voice. "I'm *not high* right now."

"Okay... and I don't have any money, since we're both just gonna sit here and lie."

Sebastien would always bring out the worst in me. I wanted to hate him for it, but he was sick. It wasn't his fault.

Addiction is a sickness. Bit by bit, that sickness was eating him. Thinking about the fire, I guess he'd been destined to be sick since he was six years old. How could he not be fucked up after everything he's been through? Sebastien might've been able to survive that night, but that sickness was gonna swallow him up sooner or later.

Of course, I struggled with knowing that I was essentially bankrolling him into an early grave. It killed me inside knowing there was nothing I could really do to save him.

"Go home, Bash. I'm not doing this with you today."

Sebastien's gonna die one day, and it's gonna be my fault. I already killed his mother, and one way or another, I'm gonna end up killing him, too.

MATH, PATIENCE, & COFFEE

MORGAN

Damien Fine is a freak of nature.

When he was fifteen, he helped his father kill his stepmother. When he was sixteen, a jury of his peers allowed him to get away with murder. When he was eighteen, some janky ass life insurance company gave him a million dollars – '*Congratulations on killing your stepmom. Step right up and get your reward*'.

He took that million dollars and built a goddamn empire.

First he was a trader on Wall Street, making bank on shorts during the 2008 Financial Crisis. Took the winnings from that and started his own hedge fund company where he profited off a bunch of failing tickers. Then at the age of twenty-nine, he started a brokerage app called Fine Investments, and by then his name had become so synonymous with riches, that millions of people couldn't wait to put their stock portfolios on their phones just because he said they should.

Everybody I know who buys stocks, does it on the Fine app. They all know the commissions line the pockets of a murderer, but most people don't care about morality so long as they see an opportunity for themselves to win. Some people don't even remember what Damien Fine did. To them, he's that guy who helped them make fifty bucks last week because they bought low and sold high on his super convenient app.

As a result, Damien Fine practically has more money than God, and it just keeps going up. *'What's your secret?'* he would always get asked by the press. While he didn't give many interviews, Damien Fine was famous for always saying the same thing every time — *"Math, patience, and coffee."*

I read it all on Wikipedia.

What a life.

On the first week of January, I interviewed at Stanford Law. On the last week of January, I received my rejection letter. In the time between those two points, Stanford Law School received an astronomical donation from the aforementioned billionaire. This reminded me of something. If my memory served correctly, it was in the middle of my last interview question that a certain Damien Fine called my interviewer.

I didn't get to finish my answer because of that call.

And then I didn't get in.

It was so clear to me then. My rejection—it was *Damien Fine's* fault. If he had never interrupted my interview, Dr. Cross could've gotten the answer to her last question.

Thinking about how important he is and how, after that donation, Stanford probably worships the ground he walks on, I had an idea. If I was going to have to apply for a second time, I was going to need something from him. A letter of recommendation. And to get it, I would need five minutes of his time to explain how he ruined my chances, and that if he wasn't the monster everybody claimed he was, he'd try to make things right. It was the least he could do.

First, I was going to have to find him.

Thankfully, he didn't make it hard.

On the corner of Southwest 15th Street and Brickell Avenue, right at the southernmost end of Downtown Miami, there was a ninety-story building that stood highest in the sky. During the day, it was a stunning structure made of mirrors and glass, glittering underneath the Florida sun. At night, the building was the brightest light in the skyline, ice blue on all of its edges with the name **FINE**, all capital letters, shining white at the top.

I could always see it on my 11th floor balcony, from thirty blocks away in the northernmost portion of downtown. For years, that bright ass building had been there, and I hardly ever paid it any mind. Not really. The city was always just a cluster of lights before. There were all kinds of names on the towers, and I'd never given any of them much thought.

Now every time I stepped outside for a cool gust of sea breeze off Biscayne Bay, all I could see was his name, written into the night sky.

When the sun would come up, I would walk thirty blocks south, all the way down to that ninety-story building, and I would sit in that first-floor lobby all morning long.

For thirty days, I planned to spend the hours between eight and noon on the first floor of the *Fine Building*. It was where his famous app was headquartered, yes, but it also housed several other unrelated businesses that Damien didn't own. They were just leasing the space.

There was a *Bank of America* that took up the entire second floor. The *Fine Building* was also home to the Miami satellite offices of *Apple*, *Google*, and *Microsoft*. Hundreds of businesses rented a piece of the beautiful tower on 15th and Brickell Ave. *Thousands* of people worked in this building.

And, of course, where there are thousands of people, there will *always* be a *Starbucks*.

It was located in the first-floor lobby, where I could see everything.

Every morning, I would sit in that coffee shop and watch the elevators.

His name is on the freakin' building, I thought. *He has to come in sooner or later.*

Every morning, I sat in the same chair, watching the same people order the same drinks. I wasn't the only regular who would sit in the shop for hours, so I didn't stick out at all. By the second week, the baristas already knew my order and they all probably just thought I was a student, coming in with my laptop to sip coffee and study.

In thirty days, I was convinced I would have what I wanted. It was a numbers game at this point. To me, it seemed highly unlikely that Damien Fine could call himself the CEO of *Fine Investments* and skip thirty days of work. So, that's how long I was willing to wait, every morning with my espresso double shot.

Because wasn't he the one that said that the secret to success was math, patience, and coffee?

———

I was sitting in the Fine Building lobby *Starbucks* for the sixteenth day in a row.

The first floor was as gorgeous as the outside. A wall of ten glass doors opened into a large lobby with glass tables and sleek transparent seats organized around a stunning rainfall fountain. Immaculately clean, the lobby always smelled like eucalyptus and expensive men's cologne, making me wonder if they were putting *Tom Ford* in the mop water.

In the early morning, the lobby was always bustling with hundreds of people in suits and dress shirts funneling in from the outside. A few of them might stop at the Starbucks before heading to one of the dozen elevators. Or some of them might meander about the pristine white lobby, pacing back and forth on their phones as they waited for their shifts to start.

I would always check each and every face.

"Espresso double shot with oat milk," Cory said my order before I could, the smile on his face getting bigger when I nodded. "M-O-R-G-A-N, right?"

"That's me," I smiled back, pulling my wallet from my tote.

The young barista was flirting with me when he said, "It's your tenth day here since I started counting. You've definitely earned a free coffee on your punch card."

"I didn't keep up with card punches, though." I shrugged regretfully.

Cory—and I was only calling him that because that's what it said on his little black nametag—held up a green business card with ten star-shaped holes. "That's okay. I did. It's on the house."

I offered him a smile, knowing that was all he'd be getting from me as a thank you. The shop wasn't busy this morning as most of the employees here would have their drinks couriered to their offices upstairs. Cory talked to me as he mixed my coffee.

"Any particular reason why you prefer to study here instead of a quieter location?"

"It smells really nice in this building." I was quick with it. Couldn't exactly say, *'I've been hoping to run into the owner of this building for more than two weeks now'*. "The eucalyptus calms me down, and once we get into first shift, the lobby becomes quiet enough."

Cory might've been around my age, tanned beige skin that made him look like he might've been mixed. There were visible acne scars on his cheeks that made him look fresh out of high school, but I'd venture to guess that he was in his early twenties.

Although he wasn't ugly, I wouldn't say he was at all my type.

Too young, too soft spoken, too Starbucks employee.

While clearly timid, he wasn't trying to be subtle about his interest with the way he repeatedly looked up and down from the drink he was making. To not make it weird, I did offer him a smile or two in response, but that's only because he was making my coffee.

In all fairness to him, it wasn't his fault that he was staring; I looked cute right now, approachable even. My hair today was new, as I took a break from my usual pixie cut and went with a shoulder length lace wig. Longer hair always makes me look friendlier than I actually am. And for that, my barista got a little too chummy for my taste.

Cory and I were alone inside. There were three people on staff, but his other two co-workers were on one of the dozens of floors, personally delivering coffee to people's offices. After coming to this shop for days, perhaps the free drink was just the excuse he needed to feel like he could—

"Do you have a boyfriend?" *How predictable.*

I wish you would've handed me my free coffee first before you asked... I could feel the shadow of tall customer appear behind me in line. Without answering Cory's question right away, I pulled my wallet out from my purse again.

"You know, I could pay for my own coffee if you feel like giving it to me for free means you can ask me that question." Behind me, I could hear one of those short exhaling laughs from the customer with the tall shadow.

Before he could respond, Cory's eyes flickered upward toward the sound, and then his back went all rigid. He didn't say anything to me or even react to what I'd just said; it all seemed like an afterthought to him now. Eyes still on the person behind me, Cory simply handed me my hot drink in complete silence. Just as I grabbed it, he began servicing the next customer, his tone more professional than it was before. "What can I get for you, Mr. Fine?"

All the muscles in my face went slack. *Did he just say?*

Of course, I didn't turn around right away. Instead choosing to sidestep around the next customer in line, using every bit of will power I had in order to not look up at him. For that reason, I only briefly saw his black sweater-clad chest, which was a blur as I hurried back to my chair at the entryway table. From my seat, I could hear his simple order and I tried to be discrete as I watched both of the men in the shop.

Cory was shooting me hard-to-read glances from behind his counter, the air around him much colder now that I'd shot down his attempt to flirt. The one he got all professional for, the one he called *Mr. Fine*—I could only see him from the back. He was tall, which was just about the only thing I could precisely determine from this angle.

He was wearing a simple black sweatshirt over what appeared to be a white t-shirt and dark wash jeans. A man that casual in building like this—even if Cory hadn't revealed his name, I might've already suspected. Frankly, he was dressed like he owned the place. The sleeves of his sweatshirt were pushed up to his elbows, revealing dark brown arms, and based off the pictures of Damien Fine that I'd seen in my research, Black Sweatshirt was even the right complexion.

Finally.

Cory was making the man's drink, and as he waited for it, perhaps he could feel my eyes on him because he turned around.

Hollywood has a bad habit of casting weird looking actors to play Damien Fine in the movie adaptations of his famous story. I guess the idea is that good looking people are harder to hate, and so even though the *real* Damien Fine is just about the most handsome man you might come across on any given day, the men who play him on screen are always hideous. You almost kind of expected him to be ugly in real life, too, but he just...wasn't.

So, perhaps this disparity was the reason I stopped breathing when he looked at me for the first time.

Of course, I knew what he looked like, but I was so used associating him with the funny looking actors that commonly portrayed him in movies, that it left me utterly unprepared when faced with the realization that I... I was *attracted* to him.

And how could I not be? He checked off all the boxes—his admirable physique stood well above six feet and even through the layers of both his sweatshirt and t-shirt, I could still the outline of firm muscles hidden underneath. It was his face that did it for me, though; his chiseled jawline, such alluringly full lips, black hair cut close to his scalp, a striking pair of brown eyes framed in thick brows, and facial hair kept neat and short over the entire lower half of his face.

I felt a drop in my stomach.

What the fuck is happening?

Photographs did not do this man justice at all, but ironically his name did, because Mr. Fine was just that... *fine*. I'm *not* in the business of giving men compliments I don't feel they deserve, so for me to be sitting there, momentarily suspended in time over how *good* this man looked—trust that it was no exaggeration.

Something that resembled recognition flashed across his handsome features, like he might've known me from somewhere, but that was impossible because as far as I knew, this was our first encounter. It wasn't until I'd realized I was ogling this man that it dawned on me that he was staring just as hard, just as frozen in place. *Why do I get the feeling that he knows who I am?*

Our little staring contest was broken up by the sound of Cory reading him his total and placing the hot coffee on the counter. And then it was like I could suddenly hear all the noise of the building again, the footsteps and chatter of worker bees navigating through their mornings.

He grabbed the cup, declining his receipt before turning toward the exit. On his way out, he briefly glanced at me, but his eyes didn't linger like they did before. The gust of wind that blew in my direction as he walked pass smelled like a vetiver-based cologne with hints of cool peppermint and warm spice. He smelled like... *Christmas*. Like expensive Christmas, but Christmas, nonetheless. I could almost be transported to the happiest moments of my childhood while breathing him in. It was so weird.

But I soon came to my senses.

You're letting him get away. That was your chance!

I could feel Cory's eyes on me as I quickly gathered my things at my table. What was he thinking of me? A woman turned him down, and now he watched her as she scrambled to catch up with another man, presumably not only because he's taller and more handsome, but also richer. *How offended Cory must feel. Unless I like spit in my coffee, I don't think I can keep coming back to this place.*

However, it wasn't lost on me that if I played my cards right today, I would never have to.

TEN MINUTES

DAMIEN

When I'm running late, I always end up having to settle for the stale espresso from the first-floor lobby Starbucks.

At least this time, the inconvenience came with a show.

The acne-scarred barista was flirting with the woman in line ahead of me. He kept glancing at her as he worked on her order, wasting precious minutes I didn't have. Cory, his name tag read, and unfortunately for me I couldn't fire him for wasting my time. I might've owned the building, but I wasn't the kid's boss. He didn't work for me—he worked for the coffee chain that paid the rent to be here.

So, all I could really do was stand in line like any other customer and watch the pitiful display. The woman in front, of course, played along because why pay full price for a cup of coffee when you can buy it with a smile? I could only make out the sides of her face from back here, but I could see why Cory was so...*distracted.*

She had a pretty side profile, a tiny head framed by pin straight shoulder-length black hair. The outward curve of her forehead ran into a satisfying slope to her nose bridge which came outward again for a cute nose, and then coming back down again for a perfectly set pout.

Cute girl, I thought. At least, from what little I could see.

There was something vaguely familiar about her, but I might've felt that way because, visually, she was my type—almond brown skin, pretty face, good height, amazing body, and there was something about her voice. It had this natural, deeper feminine rasp to it; one of those rare voices that could sound sexy reading a phone book out loud.

Why do I feel like I know her from somewhere? I couldn't shake the thought. The curiosity was unrelenting. *Turn around a little, Coffee Girl. Let me see your whole face.*

My inward encouragements were interrupted by the barista. "Do you have a boyfriend?"

Oh, for fuck's sake.

I checked the watch around my wrist. Seventeen minutes behind schedule.

Just for that, I hope she does have a boyfriend, Cory.

I had a conference call upstairs, starting in about an hour and a half and I hadn't even begun to read the sixty-page brief I'd need to brush up on before it started. The woman in front pulled a wallet form her large purse and in that sexy voice of hers, she said, "You know, I could pay for my own coffee if you feel like giving it to me for free means you can ask me that question."

Not expecting that, my eyes narrowed slightly, and before I could stop myself, I chuckled. Cory's eyes followed the sound, and in that moment, he seemed to notice that I had been waiting here for the first time. Of course, he recognized me, so it was no surprise when his posture went all stiff, the way that most people tend to tighten up around me. Without looking away from my face, he slid a cup atop the counter for the girl in front to grab.

"What can I get for you, Mr. Fine?" *And he's professional again.* The customer at the front grabbed her cup just as I ordered a simple americano. I caught just the briefest glimpse of the top half her face as she turned to walk away, her head never tilting up to get a look at me. This was unexpected. Most people would hear my name in a building like this and scramble to get a look at the infamous Damien Fine.

Coffee Girl, as it seemed, couldn't care less. Or maybe she just didn't know. But to me, it felt almost as if she could read my mind, hear my curious thoughts about why she seemed so familiar, and kept her head down for no reason other than spite. My nervous barista went on to prepare my drink, and it was while waiting that I felt eyes on me.

For that, I followed the feeling up until my eyes landed right back on Coffee Girl. She was sitting at the end of the coffee shop, those big dark eyes barely blinking, and then it hit me.

Mistress Morgan.

It didn't take me long. My memory has always been commendably sharp.

The image of her I had in my mind was that of a girl with a boy's haircut, but now she sat at the end of the coffee shop with medium length black hair, pin straight and hanging past her chin. She was prettier in person; I could own up to that. Kind of hard not to admit with the way I was staring. I might've been more discrete if she had bothered to be, but alas, she stared back, just as suspended in time as I was in that moment.

The upward curve of her mouth was subtle, the ghost of a smile in her gaze, but barely shown on her lips, like she and I already shared some sort of inside joke. A woman looks at you like that, and she's all but shouting '*approach me*' in her own quiet way. Morgan had a way of making her brown eyes look like invitations. *Come talk to me*, they said in the way her eyelids dipped, fixed on me from the other end of the shop.

But who's got the time?

"Grande americano." The barista behind the counter set my cup down for me to grab, and then the magnetism of her eyes was gone. I looked away, but I could feel the heat of her gaze linger for a moment before that went away, too. The urge to look for her again after grabbing my coffee was there, and I tried my best to fight it, but curiosity got the better of me. She was even prettier up close, I decided from the second-long look I casted her way.

And that's all it was supposed to be.

At the time, I really thought my short in-person encounter with the little dominatrix from my phone would start and end with that quick last-minute glance on my way out of a coffee kiosk.

In a far back corner of the first-floor lobby, there is a door that only five or six people have the key to. Behind that door was an elevator, ready and waiting to take a selected few to any of the other eighty-nine floors in the building, separate from general population.

There's something about elevators that makes people think that they can talk to you—and being who I am, always without fail, in every elevator there is someone with a business plan, desperate for a dollar to go with their dream. While I loved a good investment, elevator pitches weren't how I liked to come by them. For that reason, the private elevator was a must.

I got maybe six steps away from the Starbucks, hot coffee in hand, before I felt the warmth of another person following close behind me. Sometimes I don't even make it to the elevator before somebody comes at me with their idea for the next big start up. I turned on the backs of my shoes, ready to look whoever it was in the eye, turn on that 'I was on trial for murder once' charm, and calmly tell my unwanted shadow to fuck off.

What I found was Morgan.

And surprisingly, my words didn't come out as harsh.

I could feel a confused dip between my brows. "Can I help you?"

Can you help her? What the fuck are you, a cashier at Burger King? Without speaking right away, she stood there, her head of shiny black hair stopping just below my lower lip, her dark eyes bouncing as if trying to remember something she'd rehearsed. *A damn elevator pitch most likely.*

I surprised myself with what I said next. Call it curiosity, I guess.

"I'm running a little late. Can you think and walk at the same time?"

Morgan made a subtle scoffing sound like my words might've offended her, but when I turned to walk away, her footsteps behind were quick and quiet as she followed.

"I'm Morgan," she finally spoke as I waited for my elevator to come down. She didn't seem nervous, but more so careful with her words, as if she were getting ready to ask me for something I was very likely to say no to.

"I know."

Her brows dipped confusedly, a surprised squeak to her voice when she asked, "You do?"

I pointed at the white coffee cup in her hand, where her name was written in big black capital letters.

"Ohh," she made a sound of sheepish understanding, buying that this was how I knew her name already.

She was dressed comfortably—more comfortable than most people in this building—with her pale gray jogger set and white sneakers.

The get-up might've looked lazy on someone else, but the way the clothes wrapped around her figure was flattering. She looked good. She also seemed perfectly aware that I was checking her out. It didn't seem to make her all that nervous, though. There were two dimples in her cheeks that deepened as she spoke. *I think I like dimples.*

"Well, um... Mr. Fine, I was stopping you because I was wondering if you might be able to do me a favor."

The elevator interrupted her before she could tell me what that favor was.

"I gotta go to work," I replied calmly, already bored with this conversation as the doors rolled open. How boring that she'd immediately get to the point like this. Most people at least schmooze a little before they make their little requests. "To save us both some time, I'll just say no right here, and maybe you could go look for someone else to ask?" I suggested and then stepped into the empty lift. Like someone not accustomed to being told no, her features were bewildered, as if that were the last thing she expected me to say.

Funny.

"No." She slipped a foot within the gap between the elevator doors just before they could close. I pushed out a sigh, already frustrated about the time she was about to waste. "It *has* to be you."

"Look, Morgan—"

"You *owe* me," she rose her voice a little, cutting me off.

The elevator doors rolled open again, just in time, too, because now she had my attention. "I owe you? I don't even *know* you."

The only person in the world who I felt like I owed anything to, was my brother. Sometimes Martina, too.

"You owe me," Morgan repeated, and you could tell that she really believed it. My eyebrows pushed up and I nodded my head for her to spit it out. What exactly do I owe you? She explained without my asking. "Last month, I had an interview at my dream law school. Everything on my application was perfect, but in the middle of my interview, my interviewer took a call from you and wasn't able to hear my answer to an important question, and—"

"You got rejected."

She nodded, clearly a little angry with me.

This was amusing. No really. I wasn't laughing, but this was actually funny. Of all the things that could've happened today, what were the odds of *this*? Morgan stood there, her head tilted back a little to meet my eyes directly, indignant and entitled.

Entitled.

What she didn't know was that I knew all of this about her already. The interview. The rejection. The reason, even. I knew that my phone call in the middle of her interview had nothing to do with her not getting into Stanford. The irony was entertaining, to say the least. Perhaps that's why I said what I said next.

"Ride up to my floor with me?"

It would take the elevator just over a minute to reach the ninetieth floor. Morgan leaned on one side of the lift while I stood at the other. She started talking as soon as we hit the third story.

"Okay so, what I need from you is—"

"Give me a minute," I interrupted as I lifted my warm Starbucks cup in response to the confused dip of her brows. Maybe it was her line of work, but it was obvious that she had a problem with being interrupted like that. Clearly, Mistress Morgan was used to barging into people's mornings and making her demands before their first cup of coffee, but I certainly didn't have to indulge her bad habits.

She suffered through my nonchalant sips, genuinely behaving as if I was the one wasting her time. The elevator doors opened to the familiar Fine Investments corporate headquarters. To my left were dozens of offices, each commanding their own little portion of the multi-billion-dollar operation, and down a long hallway to my right, was a single office commanding over it all.

I nodded for Morgan to follow me as I turned right.

"Good morning, Mr. Fine."

"Morning, Chloe," I greeted the secretary whose desk sat perched just outside my office. Her gaze flickered over to the young stranger following behind me. Just briefly, I caught the confused squint of Chloe's brown eyes before she fixed it. If Morgan was supposed to be here today, my secretary didn't want to make it obvious that it had somehow slipped her mind.

The observation drew a barely-there smile out of me as I held the door open for my office guest. I watched Morgan's eyes widen at the skyline behind my desk, and for some reason, the subtle smile on my face grew just a little bit more. It was predictable reaction; this was the top floor of the highest building in the city. The view always makes people catch their breath when they see it for the first time.

I gave her a moment, setting my empty cup down and reaching for the thick stack of papers on my mail table. *I'm never going to finish all of this in time.*

"I need you to write me a letter of recommendation," Morgan announced, as if she couldn't see me reading. No please, no thank you, not even a question mark to imply that I had every right to refuse. I didn't look up, determined to at least finish half of the briefing before my meeting started in—I checked my phone for the time—a little over an hour.

"Did you hear me?" Her voice went up an octave. *Huh, how annoying.*

I looked up from my reading briefly, stared at her, and then went back to the stack in my hand. "No, I heard you."

"Well?" I think I heard her tapping her foot. As I read, I gave her two minutes of grace to go about her mission another way. Just before I could suggest she leave, she caught on. "Would you mind writing me a letter of recommendation?"

That's better.

"I have to know you to write about you," I replied boredly, still reading, as I walked around her to take a seat at my desk.

"Uh, okay—" she sighed, sounding rather unprepared for someone audacious enough to encroach on a man's workday. As I paged through graph after graph, the girl standing in the center of my office began to list off her credentials. "My name is Morgan Caplan. I recently graduated from The University of Miami with a 4.0. I was president of my sorority. Most people who know me would say that I'm a very hard worker with strong leadership qualities. And um..." She lost her train of thought. "And um..."

"...you own your own business," I helped as I paged through another graph.

"Right, I own my own—" She trailed off, and I truly cherished the minute-long silence before she spoke again. "Wait—how do you know that I sell hair?"

"Is that code for something?" I snorted, looking up from my stack to find her face twisted up with suspicion. "I thought you were selling...something else."

Morgan squinted, eyes studying my face before her features relaxed and she pushed out a sigh, quietly understanding.

She wasn't embarrassed, but there was something less confident about her now, mixed in with the confusion of how I could possibly know. She tucked a lock of hair behind her ear, looking like she wanted to ask.

"Someone on the admissions committee found your website during your background check," I explained to her. "You'd be surprised how some people gossip. I recognized you from the moment I saw you."

All she could do was stare at me, but there was something angry just beneath the surface of her blank expression.

"You don't need me to write you a letter of recommendation," I told her. "You just need to do a better job of concealing your—hobbies—and then maybe try applying to a different school."

"Why didn't you just tell me that downstairs?" Was her first question.

"This was funny downstairs." I shrugged. "Then we got up here and it got irritating, so unless there's anything else..." I turned to the next page in the stack of papers on my desk. "...you can see yourself out now."

I waited for the sound of my door closing. I waited for footsteps at least.

"It can't—" I heard footsteps, but they were getting closer to me instead of the door. "It can't—*can't* be a different school."

I looked up to find her directly in front of my desk, brown eyes looking down at me with burning disappointment. I leaned further back in my chair, catching the scent of her perfume. It was feminine and pleasant.

Morgan tried to mask the obvious desperation in her eyes as determination. "It *has* to be Stanford."

The first question in my mind was '*why*'. The second question was '*why is this relevant to me*'.

"You know people there, right?" she questioned before I could get a word in, her words quick and hopeful. "People on the admissions committee? That's how you know—*how you know*. Right? Tell them I'll close my site. I'll close it today. Maybe if you put in a good word for me, I could file an appeal on my rejection."

"Are you used to asking people to do things for you for no reason at all?" I had just told her that my phone call had nothing to do with her rejection. Knowing that, it was a little fascinating that she still felt comfortable enough to ask me to get involved.

Entitled.

"It's just a letter. I'll write it if you don't want to. You just have to sign it." I must've been making a face because Morgan quirked her eyebrows up, asking, "What? Do you want something from me in return?"

There was something about her tone that made me feel like she might give up a finger if I said that's what I wanted. I studied the pretty face hovering slightly above mine.

She would do anything. The subtext to her desperate question was clear. This was a girl who was willing to do absolutely anything to get what she wanted.

Anything.

I asked for the first thing that came to mind.

"I would like for you to go, so that I can get back to work."

Morgan

"So, is he gonna write the letter for you?"

Lauren was on speaker while I prepped my studio. Before every session, I liked to make sure that the space was organized and clean. As I moved about the room, disinfecting things and dusting, my sister and I were talking about my day. I had a new client due in twenty minutes. Jon Lowe—he paid for the entire night, and it was anyone's guess what I was expected to do to him for six hours straight, but a check was a check.

"I don't think so," I told my sister, trying my best to mask the exhaustion in my voice. Today was just... *a lot*. After coming home from the Fine Building, I cried for a really long time. There I was, cringing into oblivion at the thought of my website being passed around gossiping committee members behind the scenes, and hating myself for being the only person to blame for my own misfortune. Mentally, I was very tired. "He seemed really busy, so... No letter."

"How long could one letter possibly take? Sounds like an asshole," Lauren commented.

"Hmm," I made a sound of acknowledgement, unsure if I would personally use that word.

"Was he scary in person?" My sister's voice was curious. "Like—does he seem like he... you know?"

"Killed his mother and got away with it?" I began to neatly place a collection of eight different whips spaced evenly apart along the bed's red silk sheets. "I say I wouldn't know unless someone told me, to be honest. He seemed kind of..." I huffed out a sigh, fluffing some red pillows. "...*normal*, in a way. I was alone with him, and it didn't even cross my mind to be worried that he was a dangerous person. It's not like it matters—no letter regardless."

It was quiet while my sister and I slowly came to terms with my lack of options. I wished to have a closer friend who I could just unleash all my deepest secrets to—to have someone to hear about the unfortunate reason for my rejection altogether.

Lauren would just worry about me if I was honest with her. Knowing her, she'd fret over me as if I needed fixing.

And there was nothing wrong with me.

"Didn't you intern for Mayor Jean-Baptiste a few years ago?" At the sound of Lauren's random question, I paused, waiting to see where she was going with this. "Well, in case you didn't know, he's a Florida state senator now. I'm sure he'd write you a rec letter if you asked him t—"

"I'm not asking any of Mom and Dad's friends for help," I cut her off before she could finish. *I'd rather die than ask our father's best friend for favors.* If a letter from Senator Jean-Baptiste did get me into law school, the last thing I needed was for my father to feel in any way responsible. "I'll figure something else out—" There was a knock at the door. "—but right now, I have to go. I'll call you tomorrow."

Before touching the door, I pulled at the loose bow fastened around my claret silk robe, revealing a nearly sheer black lingerie set underneath. Giving the clients something nice to look at was part of the service. First rule of Mistress Morgan's dungeon—*look, but never touch.*

I opened the door and standing at the other side—to my visible astonishment—was Damien Fine. No longer wearing the clothes I'd met him in today, he was dressed in a formal suit, standing in the hallway just outside my studio, acting as if this were the most normal thing in the world. I looked around, wondering if today's client was somewhere nearby.

No. Just Damien Fine.

"I thought you said you were going to close your site today." The unexpectedness of his voice made my hand spasm at the doorknob. *Is he... is he here for...?* He spoke again and I watched his lips move, but my understanding of the words was somewhat delayed by the fact that I couldn't actually believe he was here. "How is it that I managed to book a six-hour session on a site that you supposedly closed?"

Oh wow—he really *did book the session.*

Without a word, I stepped aside and gestured for him to enter, trying not to make my movements look as nervous as I suddenly felt. Submissives don't make me nervous. At least—they're not supposed to.

I shut the door.

Damien Fine was in my dungeon, dressed in a black suit fit for a fancy gala, tailored perfectly to his toned body. Just underneath his black overcoat was a white dress shirt, long sleeves fastened all the way down to his hands. *His hands—why didn't I notice his hands before?* Large palms tipped with long fingers that I could vividly imagine wrapped wound my throat.

But wait—submissives don't get to touch my neck.

His presence in this room was so...jarring. It was like running into Barack Obama at a strip club. That clean, nostalgic scent of him just filled the space in a way that almost staked a claim to the room. As if it wasn't even mine anymore. I had to remind myself to open my mouth and speak.

"You kicked me out of your office without any indication that you would help me, so excuse me for not thinking I was being held to that." My voice was unbelievably calm considering the racing of my pulse. He was standing so close that I could feel the warmth of his body. One step closer and his chin might brush the space between my eyes. "I take it you're Jon Lowe?"

"Hmm." He nodded before shaking his head in disapproval at something. "You make it really easy to give you a fake name. And honestly—if you're going to do this whole internet prostitute thing, you should probably require some form of identification from your...johns."

I winced at the word. "I'm not a prostitute."

"That's..." His eyes trailed down my body, over my opened robe. "...debatable."

"No, I don't even—" I started to disagree, closing the sides of my robe around me. I hated that word and how I how I always felt crushed under the weight of it. He had to have heard the insecure shrill of my tone. I stopped to reel in the whininess of my voice before trying again more confidently. "I'm not a prostitute. Really, I don't sell pussy, I sell—personality."

He only blinked at first and then unsmilingly teased, "That's cute, you should put that on a T-shirt."

Brushing that off, I addressed his first point "Most people use fake names for anonymity. I don't care."

The man's eyes narrowed and his words were clipped when he commented, "It's crazy that you haven't been murdered yet then."

"What are you doing here?" I finally asked. "I didn't take you for a submissive."

He grimaced, almost offended. "Don't."

"Then *why* are you here?" I definitely sounded like I was running low on patience—because I was. For that, his head slightly tilted at the exasperation of my words, the muscles along his jaw rippling to clench and I felt a flutter in my chest. *Now what the hell was that?*

"Are you irritated by the act of somebody showing up to your job and blindsiding you? Hmm, you don't find that ironic?" His deep-voiced sarcasm was distinct. *Okay, fair point.* Even still, I didn't apologize, though he did pause and give me the room to. When it became clear that I refused, there was a twitch along the corner of his mouth—my only sign that he was trying not to smile. "I came to make you an offer. You still need my help, don't you, Morgan?"

I like the way he says my name.

I shook away the thought, and there was a long stretch of silence before the gravity of his words truly hit.

"You mean—?" For the first time in weeks, I dared to hope. Looking up to meet his eyes, I didn't allow that newfound hope to show on my face. Instead, I simply asked, "What do you want in return?"

Because I couldn't imagine that he'd do it out of the kindness of his heart.

His dark eyes dropped to my red robe once again, slow as they rose back up to my face. Parts of my body grew warm under his gaze, heating wherever he looked. I recognized that subtle wanting in his eyes, the way all men look at women they wish to completely devour. Enough men have wanted to fuck me in my lifetime for me to understand that glint in their eyes when I see it. He wasn't subtle; he wasn't trying to be.

The thought of him touching me with—those hands—didn't seem too steep a price. In fact, for Stanford, it would be a bargain.

"What do you want me to do?" I just wanted him to come outright and say it.

"Get dressed."

That was unexpected.

"If you have anything nice stashed here, I suggest you wear that." Before I could process a word, he was already halfway out the door he'd come in. His brown eyes stayed on mine, a casual confidence about his gaze with his parting words. This man already knew I would follow him out. "I saw a lounge downstairs on my way up. I'll wait ten minutes."

SOMETHING TERRIBLE

MORGAN

Lorraine's on Biscayne was a little bar on the first floor of the building where I received clients.

The ground floor lounge was an outdoor space, walled with tall wood panels on all four sides, to give it an indoor feel. The fence was covered in climbing vines, wrapped around each plank, and blooming with the small white flowers of late Florida winter. There were eight patio tables evenly spaced out along a concrete foundation, all directly across an outdoor bar and DJ booth that played contemporary jazz.

Like tonight, for instance, an instrumental jazz cover of a familiar song played lightly in the background as I opened the entry gate into the main courtyard. I didn't immediately spot him sitting at the table on the far end of the lounge. But it was as if I could feel his eyes on me almost instantly, parts of my skin heating in places where I assumed his eyes lingered.

I followed that heat all the way to the back of the courtyard, where he sat, a crystal glass of something brown resting in his hand. As the space between us shrank, I watched as his eyes scanned the black dress I was wearing now. The dress was the nicest thing I owned in the dungeon closet, and whatever he needed me to be so dressed up for would have to take it or leave it.

"Your hair was longer this morning."

I shrugged, not particularly interested in explaining the logistics of invisible lace right now. While Morgan Caplan liked to be creative with her hair, Mistress Morgan exclusively rocked a pixie cut. Damien Fine just so happened to catch me during work hours.

"After you kicked me out of your office, I lost my good sense and cut it all off."

A lazy smile broke through, lighting up his features. He was very handsome, I reluctantly thought. Especially in that suit. Before I could admire him for too long, I took the opposite seat and cut straight to the chase.

"What do you want from me?"

"You shouldn't ask that way. It's a mutually beneficial agreement, I promise." He sounded like he was teasing me before asking, "What are you drinking?"

"I don't drink."

Damien's brows pulled together, somewhat unconvinced. But it was the truth, and even if I did drink, I would want to be sober for this. My ears were still hot off the words *'mutually beneficial agreement'*.

He spoke again, gesturing his drink in my direction. "You need a huge favor, right?" To his question, I gave a tight nod. "I'm prepared to help you if you do something for me in return."

I exhaled slowly before asking, "And what's that?"

"Whatever I say." He finished that vague requirement with a set time. "One month."

"Whatever you say?" I almost spat back the words. It was far too open ended for my liking. "That could mean anything. I'm not comfortable with—"

"Interesting." He chuckled and then asked in that condescendingly deep voice of his, "Would it make you more comfortable if I used a word you're more familiar with?" To my confused features he simply said, "Submissive."

If I had been drinking something, it would've been sputtered all over the small black table. Initially outraged, I opened my mouth to retort, but then quickly shut it, remembering the contract I would have all my clients sign before coming into my dungeon.

'My word is law. When you consent to be my submissive, you do whatever I say.'

Damien booked an all-night session and those exact words were in my contract. He seemed like the type to read everything before signing. Damien wasn't asking anything of me that I hadn't asked of others at least one hundred times.

"I don't sub. I've never been a submissive in my life." This confession seemed to amuse him further. In fact, it might've made making me submit feel like more of a conquest for him. I wanted to wipe that smirk clean off his face. "I always dom. That's my role. That's my comfort zone. We can do *that*. I could go easy on you if—"

"Yeah, that's not gonna happen." He didn't let me finish that thought, polishing off the last of the brown in his glass, his words final and dripping with *'you got me fucked up'*. "I'm sure you've seen enough people sub in your lifetime. You'll figure it out."

"I don't think I want—"

"This BDSM thing is yours—not mine," he pointed out. "Unlike you, I don't have a dozen whips in some windowless torture chamber hidden away somewhere. If you're gonna sub for the first time in your life—wouldn't you rather do it with someone far less creative than you seem to be?"

I opened my mouth, but then closed it. Points were being made. If I was going to be a sub, someone green to the world of BDSM would be the easiest way. He *was* making sense.

"You've never been a dominant before?"

"It doesn't seem like it'd be hard." His words were clipped, that kind of terse masculine dismissiveness that I hated. Men think they know everything. "The paperwork I signed to meet you tonight. How about you switch out your name for mine, print it out, and bring the contract to my apartment tomorrow night? Fair?"

More than fair, I thought to myself, knowing my terms were very reasonable. "And tonight? You wanted me all dressed up because?"

Some sort of test ride perhaps?

Maybe he liked his women to look polished before ravishing them. The theory sent a buzzing between my legs, and I hated the little part of me that grew excited at the thought of being ravished by this man. I hated that he was handsome. I hated that he smelled so good. I hated his stupid, perfect hands.

All my fantasies—ideas—came to a screeching halt at the utterance of his next few words.

"An ice breaker of sorts. There's a charity benefit that I have to attend tonight," Damien replied, then pointed at the expensive-looking watch strapped around his brown wrist. "In fifteen."

My brows came together when I realized. "So, a date?"

"Whatever I say, right?"

The FEEL Center is a non-profit organization in the heart of Downtown Miami.

Everyone in Miami knows that The FEEL Center is where they send the sob story kids. At least once or twice a year, there'd be some tragic piece in the local news about neglectful parents damn near killing a child, and everyone in town would collectively sigh in relief at an announcement that, that child was being sent to FEEL.

That little center tucked between the towering downtown high rises, with its tall gates and big playground out back, worked miracles. You just knew children were safe there. I'd never been inside of FEEL, but I would drive past it daily.

It was Damien Fine, of all people, who held open the door and invited me in for the first time.

There was a fundraiser this evening. According to Damien, all of the kids were on some sleep-away trip to DC.

And now the building was filled with guests in cocktail attire, mingling in the main lobby of the center. My little black dress didn't blend well in the dozens of women dressed in flowy gowns, but my pixie cut was neat, and when Damien told me where we were going, I was able to do my make up in the car.

I didn't look terrible. And Damien struck me as the type of person to tell me to my face if I did.

I must've been presentable enough, because his hand was settled at the small of my back, making us look way more intimately acquainted than we actually were. Like he was proud to call me his date, and he wanted everyone in attendance to know that I was his tonight. My skin buzzed warm where I could feel the weight of his hand. I tried to ignore it.

"Damien!"

An absolutely stunning woman floated into view, wearing a flowy white dress that made her look nothing short of an angel. She greeted my date like she hadn't seen him in years. "You're finally in the building again. What has it been—two years?"

Ahh, apparently it *had* been years.

"Caprice," Damien greeted her warmly—at least, his best attempt at it. The man holding my back didn't have a fraction of the warmth Miss Caprice had.

She was a tall woman—might've been about five-ten without her glittery heels on—two inches taller than me. Her hair was in a sleek black bun, with two curls on either side of her head framing her face. As if feeling me looking at her, her big brown eyes slid down to me, the smile on her face never faltering.

Damien introduced me, equally as warm as before, "This is Morgan."

"So, *you're* the reason I can't sell him off tonight." I had no idea what she was talking about, so I stared at her blankly before confusedly shrugging. "Wow—you're just about as talkative as Damien is."

This was supposed to be funny, I think, so I laughed and used my context clues to simply reply, "Sorry, Damien's not for sale."

"No hard feelings, Morgan," she nodded, peering up at him again. Her smile was as bright and as white as her dress. She was so happy to see him—it made me wonder why I was his date and not her. We had a lot of the same attributes—dark brown skin, brown eyes, tall heights, pretty faces. "I wouldn't sell mine either."

Oh, so she has someone already. Poor Damien; she's very lovely. I could admit that to myself now that I knew she likely wasn't pining after the man beside me; now that I noticed her ring finger for the first time and clocked her massive, crystal-clear diamond. Whoever she was with may not have been a billionaire, but he was certainly well off. I snuck a quick glance at Damien to see if the reminder bothered him at all. His expression hadn't changed.

The two friends had a short, pleasant conversation that I tuned out as I scanned the room. So many of the men in the room were abnormally tall, and when I recognized one of them to be Miami Heat all-star Shaun Taylor, it was a safe bet to assume that many of the towering men in the room were basketball players, too.

And just like Caprice's diamond ring, now that I knew what to look for, I began noticing the familiar flaming basketball logo of the Miami Heat all around the room. This was some kind of FEEL Center, Miami Heat joint event.

Why was Damien here? Did he have some kind of connection with the team? As rich as he was, I wouldn't be surprised if he owned the team. I'd never paid enough attention to sports to know those kinds of things.

Just as I returned to Damien and Caprice's conversation, it seemed she was gearing up to leave us now. Before she went, she pulled two champagne flutes off a traveling serving tray and handed them to us. She left me with the parting words, "It was so nice meeting you, Morgan."

When we were alone, I peered up at Damien from the top of my champagne glass, feeling a faint smile growing on my lips. "What were you two talking about? I got distracted."

"My contribution tonight," he replied coolly.

"How much?"

"The difference." There was a quirk between my brows. To my confusion, he explained. "They have a fundraising goal to reach tonight. If they fall short, I fill the gap."

"What's the goal?"

Damien's brown eyes wandered above my head, and I followed his gaze to a decorative banner that read, *Annual F.E.E.L. Center Charity Week. Tonight's goal: Five million.*

"That's very generous of you," I marveled as I read the number. I turned around and met his face again. "Are you doing this because you're in love with Caprice?"

"What?" his tone was genuinely taken aback, as though he had no idea why I might think such a thing. He tossed the glass of champagne down like a shot of tequila. "She's engaged."

"That's not exactly a no. And she's very pretty. You seem to like her a lot."

"I *do* like her a lot, but it's not like that," Damien denied all my little theories. "Caprice is just very... sweet. She's more like a sister."

I pulled a skeptical eyebrow up, wondering if Damien went around giving millions of dollars to everyone he found sweet.

"She's one of the kindest people I know. From my experience, a person doesn't get to be that kind unless something terrible has happened to them."

In my mind, I disagreed with him a little. People with terrible life experiences don't always come out nicer for it.

"So, I'm not here to make her jealous?"

"No." He sounded like he might laugh. "You're here because I told her I couldn't take part in some date auction. She's stuck auctioning off dates with ball players tonight instead."

"You told her you had a girlfriend to get out of it," I smiled at the thought, but then wondered why a man like Damien didn't just have a real girlfriend to hide behind. "I'm your girlfriend tonight, aren't I?"

"Naturally."

"Hmm," I thought, remembering his hand on my back from before, wondering when he had managed to slip it away without my noticing. Was it while he talked to his friend? I made conversation to distract myself from the disappointed buzz in my stomach. "So, does Caprice own the FEEL Center?"

Damien smiled a little, something about my question amusing him. "Yes—in a way. It was her idea."

"Oh, so she doesn't just dress like one, she *is* an angel."

"She acts like one, too," Damien added fondly, chuckled, and then very seriously added, "Not my type."

Briefly, I wondered what his type might be.

"Do you want mine?" I asked him suddenly, gesturing to my untouched champagne flute. "I'm not really a fan of champagne."

He set his glass down on the lobby counter behind us, taking mine off my hands. There was a stack of FEEL Center brochures beside his empty flute and I curiously picked one up. He drank my champagne as I read to myself.

*The FEEL center is a pediatric psychiatric care facility in Downtown Miami founded by four colleagues from The University of Miami—Damien **F**ine, Logan **E**zra, Rebecca **E**mison, & Caprice **L**atimore.*

My eyes snapped up from the paper mid-passage. To me, it became clear that Damien wasn't paying the difference for the fundraiser because he liked Caprice. He was giving that much because this place—it was just as much his as it was hers. Damien Fine is a co-owner of one of the most effective non-profits in the city; he has saved hundreds of children and counting.

His hand was at my back again and something in my chest jumped. It was impossible to ignore this time.

"Find anything interesting?" Damien asked in response to what could only be the expression on my face. Studying his features, there was a softness behind his brown eyes that I suspected I could only see because he was on his fourth drink of the evening. It was something about him that I got the feeling he tried very hard not to show, because maybe once upon a time, that softness spelled trouble for him. So he buried it beneath unsmiling features, beneath a practiced nonchalance, deep deep underneath that intimidating exterior.

But right now—just in that moment—I thought I *really* saw him.

To his expectant gaze, I replied, "I think by your logic, something terrible must've happened to you, too."

EQUALS

MORGAN

The main lobby of the Cygnus Tower was an off-white cream color with gold accents.

The set up was opulent with a clean, modern luxury .

This morning, I received a text message with a six-digit passcode and instructions on how to find the private elevator directly to the penthouse suite.

Of course, Damien Fine would have his own private elevator in his apartment building, too. I was rolling my eyes as I punched in the numbers, thinking about how Damien must've felt like he was too good to ride up to the eightieth floor with the rest of the riff raff living in the Cygnus Tower.

I could feel the front desk attendant's eyes on my back as I waited for the elevator to come down. There I was, standing in this high-class Miami lobby in strappy black heels and a black trench coat. The only people who wear trench coats in this hot ass city are drug dealers and escorts. I wondered which of those two the spectators on the ground floor assumed I was. In my hands, I held a thirty-page contract, each page initialed with a cursive MC, and the confidence of the signature grew progressively humble down the stack.

I couldn't believe it had come to this, swallowing the last bit of my pride before stepping into the small, metallic box.

It was his private elevator, so it was no surprise that the steel-walled lift with the intricate light fixture, smelled just like him; black pepper and vetiver, with just a hint of peppermint. In all honesty, I could drown blissfully in his scent, which I did when the double doors behind me shut.

Like the lobby, the lighting in the elevator was warm, washing my brown skin in a light gold that made my complexion shimmer. I had spent a significant amount of time getting ready for him this evening. Shower, wax, shower again, moisturize, full make up, and a clean floral scent. He had better appreciate it.

The elevator doors opened out to a long hallway, and at the end was a white door. My heels clicked against the off-white marble floors that shined so clean, I could see my reflection in them. Above the door's threshold was a number in painted gold—8001—the only unit on this floor.

I knocked twice before the door disappeared underneath my fist.

There he stood, a plain white shirt and black joggers, wordlessly stepping out of my way before motioning me inside. The front door shut just as I turned, extending the signed contract toward him. His eyes on me were desirous, bold in the way they expressed how much he wanted me, unashamed to be obvious.

It would've made me feel so powerful if I was the one in control.

"Did you make any changes?" he asked as though he knew I would.

"Just one," I confessed before explaining, "I make my clients call me Mistress. The male equivalent is Master. I'll call you whatever you want me to call you—except that."

He chuckled. "Master and Mistress hit different, don't they? It would make me uncomfortable, too. You can call me Mr. Fine."

I nodded, a little bit dejected that he wasn't allowing me to use his first name. Not that I didn't understand. I would never let a submissive call me by my name. As a first-time dominant, though, I expected him to be a little more lenient with that. I think he let me call him Damien last night—but then again, last night I was pretending to be his girlfriend.

He was different than before, but before there had been no paperwork between the both of us. The ice was sufficiently broken; I'd seen enough of him to know that I would be safe here alone, but now he was reeling back, enforcing some distance so that I would be sure to know what my place was.

I *wasn't* his girlfriend.

I was his submissive.

"There's a bathroom down that hall." He pointed as he spoke in clipped syllables, not a trace of warmth or softness in him now. "Go on in there and wash that stuff off your face."

Anger burned hot at the back of my neck at first, and I looked away from him quickly or else he might see the fire blaze behind my eyes. I couldn't afford to let my temper ruin my second chance. One day down, twenty-nine more to go. I could do this.

I could swallow my pride and just do as I was told for once.

It would all be over soon.

I looked at him again and nodded once. He seemed a little amused, no doubt recognizing how hard that little head nod was for me. A good submissive would've said the words '*Yes, Mr. Fine,*' but I feared my tongue might burst into flames if I could ever stoop so low.

In the bathroom, my breathing was rough and quickened as I tried to keep my anger under control. Hours—I'd spent hours getting ready for this evening—at least forty-five minutes on my make up just for him to make me wash it off.

I stared at the girl in the mirror. Natural wet face, chest heaving with panting, furious breaths. She could be as angry as she wanted in this sterile powder room, but when she walked out, she would be the picture of submission. The girl in the mirror wore a simple black mid coat that stopped just above her knees, tied tightly around her waist with a matching belt. Almost all of the buttons were fastened, except for two at the top which exposed a hint of pastel purple lace underneath.

It was the only piece of lingerie that I owned that wasn't dominatrix black.

The girl in the mirror's features were fraught with worry, the question of how long she would get to keep her coat on shining in her eyes.

She was about to cry.

Fuck, I thought, mentally giving her a pep talk. *You just got here. You are not going to let him see you like this. Pull yourself together, Morgan. You are doing what you have to do, but don't you forget who you are.*

Brave face. Brave face. Brave face.

Damien's apartment was spacious. A large central kitchen, all white everything except for the stainless-steel appliances. Off to the side, was a casual dining room, where I assumed he would take his coffee in the mornings, and just behind that was a living room twice the size of my entire apartment. Three hallways lead away from the kitchen where I presumed one could find at least half a dozen ridiculously huge bedrooms.

He was standing in the dining room when I walked out of the bathroom.

"Better," was all he said when he looked over my now clean face. My steps toward him were slow and borderline reluctant. Especially now that I could see the print of his dick outlined in his joggers. If I wasn't anxious before, I certainly was now.

Because what the *entire* fuck was I supposed to do with that? Seriously. When it comes to dick, there are essentially five size designations. There is small, average, above average, big, and disrespectfully big.

Disrespectfully big dick is so named because only a disrespectful ass motherfucker would think it is acceptable to use such a dick on another human being. Disrespectfully big dick is a weapon. As far as I was concerned, Damien Fine was about to pull a semi-automatic rifle out on me, so I stopped getting any closer. Mr. Fine was a statistical outlier—big beyond reason. Almost any man that comes in after him may know that someone bigger had come before.

Perhaps this was why he had to bribe women into letting him touch them.

"Take the coat off." My body betrayed me a little bit, because there was something about the timbre of his voice that sent aroused chills up my spine. In that tone of voice, he could tell me to undress as often as he wanted and the only response he'd get out of me was an undone knot at my waist and swift removal of my coat every single time.

Of course, I'd never tell him that.

"Bend over."

I almost stuttered. "Over what?"

Gone was the obedience from just a few short seconds ago.

His eyes gestured to the dining room table, and I watched him closely as her circled around to my back. I scoffed softly, but stepped closer to the dark wood table and just looked, putting on a brave face. Behind me, I could feel him standing, waiting, just close enough so that the fabric of his shirt lightly kissed the skin of my bare shoulders. "So what? Am I not good enough for that royal bed of yours?"

I could feel the wind of his quiet exhaling laugh behind my head. Feeling his breath against my skin sent humiliating goosebumps all along the nape of my neck and shoulders. I wondered if he could see them. Did he think they were from arousal or fear? Truthfully, I didn't even know the answer myself.

I felt the warmth of his hand settle at the base of my neck. If he couldn't see my goosebumps, he could certainly feel them. Slowly, he guided my head down until one side of my face pressed into the cold wood of his dining room table. I could see my breath fogging cloudy shapes against the dark brown surface, the time between each exhale growing shorter and shorter.

I was hyperventilating.

"Are you—" His deep voice startled me and I flinched, which interrupted him for a moment before he tried again. "Are you about to cry?"

"No," I replied to the disbelief in his tone, sounding very much like I was.

"Get up," he said quietly, so quietly that I wasn't sure if it was my hopeful mind playing tricks on me. When he said it a second time, I knew it was over. "Get up."

I was so relieved. He sounded annoyed, but beneath it there was some semblance of patience, too. When I didn't move fast enough, I felt his hand wrap around the front of my neck and pull me up harshly.

Damien circled around to an adjacent side of the table.

"Look up," he gave me permission to look at him and when he found my eyes, he bluntly asked, "When was the last time you let somebody fuck you?"

I swallowed. "My junior year."

"So, three years ago?"

"Of high school," I clarified.

He only blinked, and the simple math must've been automatic for a genius like himself. Nearly seven years. "Hm—maybe you *were* selling personality after all," he mused. I didn't smile. "You've never been with a man before."

"I'm not a virgin—"

"Unless you were messing around with grown men when you were in high school, what I say stands—you've never been with a man before. Boys, maybe, but not men."

"I've been with *plenty* of men. Hundreds of them," I told him if only just to make him squirm. He didn't even flinch. "They've just never been with *me.*"

"And with all that experience, you cry at the thought of one touching you." This little observation was amusing him, but I couldn't see what was so funny. Before his mockery could embarrass me, I got angry instead.

"You are *fucking* humongous." I said it as an insult; he took it as a compliment. "It's going to hurt and—and—"

"And, and?"

"I don't want it to hurt." My voice was meek, a whining whimper I wasn't used to hearing from myself. It was embarrassing enough to be afraid; it was even more humiliating to be afraid of a man.

Men are supposed to fear *me*, not the other way around.

"Living room." He nodded in that direction, dismissing me. The further away from the table I got, the easier it was to breathe. He didn't follow me, which also made it easier to breathe as the distance between us increased. I took a seat on the cloud soft sectional, sinking into its pillowy white cushions. Briefly, I found myself marveling at how this man's couch was more comfortable than any bed I've ever slept on.

From behind me, further away as if he were now standing in the kitchen, I heard him call out an order.

"Take everything off. Be naked by the time I get there."

I turned to find him standing by his refrigerator, filling a water glass at the dispenser. "On the couch?"

"Sure."

He didn't seem to care about someone planting their bare pussy on the stark white fabric of his probably bazillion-dollar furniture. If I made any sort of mess, he was likely to throw it out and buy a new one. The absurdity of the thought made me laugh a little.

I didn't know how much time I had before he'd join me in the living room, so I was quick as I unclasped my bra and slid down my panties. I could hear him opening a cabinet in the kitchen before he said, "I'm going to make you a cup of tea."

'*I'm going to make you a cup of tea*', he says, not '*Would you like a cup of tea?*' Obviously, I have no choice in the matter.

I turned my head to find him pouring the water in his glass into an electric kettle. On the kitchen island was a small lavender-colored tin and a single glass mug.

I asked, "Why?"

Was he trying to drug me?

He lifted the box and read, "It's a patented blend of chamomile, valerian, and peppermint." His eyes flickered up to meet mine and he reasoned, "Good for anxiety."

"And you use this to calm down all of your nervous hoes?"

He smiled before shaking his head. "None of my hoes have ever been this nervous."

Damien opened the tin and pulled out a single teabag. It was one of those fancy brands of tea, where the bag was made of thin cloth instead of paper.

"So why do you have the tea on hand then?" I asked.

"It helps me sleep sometimes," he answered, revealing more about himself than he realized. He has trouble sleeping. A man doesn't go out and buy tins of obscure fancy tea for one or two bad nights of sleeplessness. No. For him, it must be chronic.

"Will it make me go to sleep?" I asked as the water in the kettle came to a boil.

"Only if you let it. For you, it'll just relax your muscles, make you a little less tense."

"Right. Someone like you would need me to be as loose as possible, I'm sure." He laughed, again taking what was meant as an insult as a compliment instead.

I watched as he poured the hot water into the glass mug, watching as the clear water slowly turned caramel. With the cup, he walked to the dispenser side of his refrigerator, placed the steaming mug under the receiver, pressed a button and waited for a single ice cube to drop into the tea, making sure it wouldn't be scalding hot by the time he handed it to me.

I looked at the mug in my hand now, the steam rising from it smelling absolutely lovely. He didn't wait or hover around waiting for me to taste it. Instead, he walked the opposite side of his living room where he kept a small bar of four full bottles of brown liquor and two crystal glasses. From reading the bottle, I could tell that he was pouring bourbon into the cup in his hand.

"You still don't drink, right?" he asked me, remembering my reservations from the night before.

"Right." I took a sip of my tea. It tasted just as lovely as it smelled. I liked it, smiling a little before I realized I could still feel his eyes on me. I met his gaze from far. "Why am I naked?"

For someone who had ordered me naked, he was barely even looking at me. Most men devour you with their eyes at the first sign of naked skin. He was acting as if my nakedness in his living room were the most mundane thing in the world. A little part of me might've wanted him to lust... maybe just a little bit.

Damien finished the last of the drink in his glass, setting it upside down onto the bar surface before walking toward me. He took a seat on the coffee table across from me, close enough that I could smell him now. I caught that familiar scent of him from the elevator, and coached myself not to lean toward it.

"Because I own you and I told you to be," he answered simply. "Drink."

And I did. Not out of obedience, I told myself, but because I liked the taste. *You don't own me*, I wanted to tell him. In twenty-nine days, I would have what I wanted and I could carry on with life, pretending that he never existed.

He reached for my cup after I'd emptied it, asking, "How do you feel now?"

I said the only honest word that came to mind. "Better."

He almost smiled at that.

"Scoot up to the edge of the couch for me." The man spoke it like a suggestion, but I knew it was an order, just like everything else he'd tell me to do was an order. I was at the edge of the couch in seconds, close enough to him that our knees were touching. That didn't last long because he got down on the ground, which I found disorienting because I had never gotten down on my knees for a submissive.

But I realized that he did it so that he could be eye level with my more intimate regions. Very slowly, he personally separated my knees, taking in every bit of me with his eyes.

"You're pretty down here, too," he complimented. Damien had a way of offering praise without ever seeming like his intent was to flatter. He could say things like *you have a pretty pussy* in exactly the same way you'd expect someone to say, *today is Saturday*.

Nevertheless, I felt something flutter in my stomach anyway.

Curiously, he asked, "How many men have tasted it?" When I didn't answer right away, he looked up to meet my eyes and guessed, "Hundreds?"

I shrugged. "Possibly."

He only squinted. "And you showered before you came over, right? Thoroughly?"

He didn't mean it as an actual question, but more as a snide comment.

Fuck you. The words were bitten on my tongue. Submissives do not swear at their dominant.

"Of course."

"Lay back for me," he instructed, and then as an afterthought he mentioned, "And no matter how good it may feel, do *not* touch the back of my head, do you understand?"

I didn't think it was possible, but apparently there is a way to make someone feel like *your* bitch despite having your head between their legs. What little power I thought I might've had because he was the one performing on me—*gone*.

"Do you understand?" he asked again. Slower the second time, like I was stupid.

"I understand."

I felt his thumb first. I knew it was his thumb because I could feel his other four long fingers resting comfortably on my pelvis. I took in a sharp breath, hating that I liked his touch, hating how quickly I was moving on from being spoken to in that way. He'd been looking for my sweet spot, and by the sound of the gasp that sliced through the silence of his apartment, we both knew he found it.

It seemed the entire evening was forgiven the moment his tongue pushed against me, replacing his finger, expertly starting from the base, and rolling upward. I arched my back so reflexively, it could've snapped.

This was more than I'd be willing to do for any submissive. This was *intimate*.

Reflex would've immediately had my hands at the back of his head, desperate to hold him closer, aching to press him harder against my body. Instead, my hands were at my heating breasts, holding them at their hardening peaks as the rest of my body warmed.

Ahh, yes.

Just like that.

I wanted to encourage him, but that would make the intimate exchange all the more intimate, and just the thought made me uncomfortable. One of his hands traveled upward to replace mine at my breasts, multitasking my stimulation as his tongue went to work harder against my sensitive skin. You couldn't tell me that he wasn't trying to grind me to dust, to force the encouragements out of me. My fingers dug into the white cushions of the couch, surrendering that first moan like a fallen soldier.

"*Yes...*"

I only thanked God I didn't say his name. My pride might've never recovered.

I swore I could feel him smile against me, the sound of my whiny-voiced abandon no doubt stroking his ego in all the right ways. I wondered if he was fully erect now. I wondered if we might try again. Even in spite of the inevitable pain, the thought of him holding me at my waist underneath his body, moving us against this couch—I didn't hate it. It would be better than the table.

"*Please...*" I moaned when he licked me again, his other hand diving two large fingers into me with relative ease from how wet I was. His perfect lips closed around my clit, and just like the monster he turned out to be, he sucked on me gently, turning my whimpering moans into full on cries, pleading for him to stop, pleading for him to not stop. I had no idea what I wanted. No idea what was happening.

I was teetering the fine line between sanity and insanity, and he seemed utterly determined to have me lose my mind. My thighs were quaking, unsure of whether they might close to push him out or close to keep him there.

Damien pushed in and out of me, tongue licking at various pressures and rhythms just above his penetrating fingers. My arched back rose further and his hand at my breast lowered to push me back down, holding me to the couch cushions as he deepened his assault on my senses, leaving me nowhere to run. Pressure mounted quickly now that I couldn't squirm. I whispered pleas to deaf ears, knowing that the more desperate I sounded, the more encouraged he was.

Only when I felt like I might explode did I say his name—his *first* name—shouted so loudly, I was grateful that he didn't have neighbors. And I came. I came so hard that I ruined his couch, though it took me a moment to realize because that had never happened to me like that before. I didn't know I was a squirter. My submissives ate me out like servants serving their mistress, void of confidence, void of that raw male prowess. Damien ate me like he had a goal in mind.

A goal reached, I presumed, from the look of accomplishment in his eyes as he looked over my quivering body, the first time this evening that he seemed to take in my nakedness with any semblance of desire. That same desire from last night. Some part of me was calmed to see it again.

"What's your safe word, Mistress Morgan?" Unlike the men before him, it didn't sound submissive when he called me that. His tone was harmlessly mocking, as if to say, *look how the mighty have fallen*. At least—I was taking it that way.

"Vanilla," I answered, watching him closely as he hovered inches above me, knowing what was coming next. I wondered if I might use my safe word on the first night. From the size of him, it wasn't lost on me that this might feel like losing my virginity all over again. *How courteous of him to make sure I was as wet as possible before trying again,* I thought sarcastically. "Can I ask you something, Mr. Fine?"

Unlike him, I sounded very much like a submissive when I called him that.

Sometimes it's easier if you distract yourself with something, so I tried to make conversation, stiffening a little bit when I felt his hardness against my opening. He didn't push in immediately, instead replying, "Ask."

"Why couldn't I touch the back of your head when you—"

"Because that would make us equals," he interrupted simply, lips so intimately close to mine that his words felt like a kiss. "When you grab the back of my head, you imply that you have a say on how this goes. Don't ever misunderstand, Mistress Morgan. You don't have a say about anything here. You can use your safe word if you need it, but we are never going to be equals."

And in one swift motion, he pushed into me. My mind split and I saw stars before the lights of his ceiling took me up and swallowed me whole, leaving my vision suspended in white nothingness as I worked my way down from blinding pain and pleasure all mixed into one.

MY FATHER

DAMIEN

Morgan was still asleep in the guest room when I woke that morning.

Shortly after getting out of bed, I checked in on her and found her wrapped in plush white sheets all the way up to her naked shoulders. Last night had taken a lot out of her. When she said she hadn't been with anyone for close to seven years, despite her line of work, I believed her.

It was even more believable when I could see for myself how much pain she was in; feel for myself how tightly her body wrapped around me. No matter how gentle I could've been, there was really nothing I could do to make things completely painless for her. It just wasn't feasible. The only way was to bite the bullet and simply get it over with. It would be better for her the second time; relatively painless by the fourth or fifth time.

Morgan slept through breakfast, slept through through the loud machines of the maid cleaning the mess we made of the living room, slept through lunch.

I was in my home office when Morgan finally woke up. Wrapped in a white blanket, she appeared at the threshold at a very coincidental moment. At that time, I just so happened to have her *Mistress Morgan* website loaded onto my computer, reading the error page.

Error 404: *This website does not exist.*

"Can I borrow one of your shirts?" she asked and then yawned, leaning against the threshold between my office and the rest of the penthouse. She walked all the way over here on her own; that was a good sign. I hadn't hurt her too bad.

"Yeah, I'll get you one in a minute."

"I left my coat on the floor in the dining room," she told me, walking further into the office. I watched her slow steps from behind my desk, noting that she walked like someone who must've felt sore. "I can't find it anymore."

"I gave it to the maid to be cleaned with the rest of the laundry."

"Well, what am I supposed to do go home in?" she questioned.

"You're not going home," I told her, only having decided this after seeing how sore she woke up this afternoon. She should stay in and heal a bit. "You owe me thirty days. You didn't think I was going to let you spend most of it across town, did you?"

Morgan stared, brown eyes on me completely stoic for a moment before she sighed and forced a smile, trying to seem unfazed. "I take it this means you like me."

I almost smiled, curiously wondering, "Is there a reason why you've been practically celibate for over six years?"

Morgan's forced smile turned sly before she asked, "Would it make you feel like a piece of shit if I said I was saving myself for my wedding day?"

"Yes," I answered. "But I don't believe that."

"When I was eighteen, I met a guy who, once a week, would pay me five hundred dollars to stomp on his balls—" I cringed. "—and since then, I've just never had to do the whole sex thing. I do what works for me instead."

"The whole sex thing," I amusedly repeated. "You make it sound like sex is something that is done *to* you instead of *with* you."

She rolled her eyes. "Says the man who did it *to* me, and not *with* me, last night."

"I tried not to make it hurt."

"I couldn't tell," she bit back.

If I had been any gentler, we would've practically been making love.

"You could've safe worded out if it was really that painful." Morgan only shrugged at this, and I got the feeling that the only reasons she didn't safe word out last night was her pride. "Are you okay? I can see that you're walking a little—"

"I'm fine." Morgan shrugged with a shake of her head. Her voice was light and carefree as she assured, "No need to call a doctor and tell them you've got a big dick."

Her blunt sense of humor caught me off guard. I choked on a laugh, but then masked it with the clearing of my throat. A subject change was needed, and I could see that Morgan took that as a win.

"You should write down your measurements. I can get my assistant to pick up some clothes for your stay."

Her eyebrows came together. "I don't even get to choose what I wear this month?"

"Chloe doesn't pick out the clothes—a stylist does. She's just going to show up with a rack or two," I explained. "You choose what you want from the racks, send the rest back. It's how I do my shopping."

"Fancy," was all she said, walking around the cramped office, running her hand along the spines of the various books I kept on hand. The white sheet from her bed trailed on the cedarwood floors at her bare feet. "I like your office. It's very cluttered."

I grimaced. "Are you making fun of me?"

"No." She shook her head earnestly. "You just step into an office like this and think—wow, I bet a lot of work gets done in here. Look at your desk; all those papers and folders and—"

"Ideally, a lot of work should be getting done in here. When I'm not *distracted*," I hinted.

"I love messy desks. They make me feel safe some-how." She didn't get the hint, continuing to walk around the office, fingering the bookshelves, stopping directly in front of a little brown box on the third shelf. Before I could tell her not to touch it, it was already in her hands. "What's this?"

"My father."

Morgan was surprised before visibly cringing, guiltily setting the old cardboard box back where she'd found it. "I'm sorry, I didn't kno—"

"It's fine—"

"It's just, I didn't know people kept their family members in boxes like this—"

"He wasn't exactly a cherished member." I gestured to the brown leather armchair across from my desk. "Maybe you should sit down before you touch anything else you're not supposed to. I'm gonna go get you a shirt."

Moments later, Morgan was seated across from me in silence, watching me work in a black t-shirt of mine. It fit her like a short dress, and she hadn't even bothered leaving the office to put it on. For these next few weeks, her body was barely her own anyway. No need faking the modesty, she must've figured. Morgan had allowed me exactly eighteen minutes of unencumbered silence, watching me work, before she broke the productive quiet once again.

"You hated him?"

I stopped typing, looking over my desktop to find her still seated, thin fingers combing through her short hair, brown eyes blinking expectantly.

"Who?"

"Your father," she replied like the answer was obvious, and I tried to multitask as she continued. "That's why you haven't bothered buying him an urn, right?"

"Do you usually let your submissives interrogate you like this?"

"My submissives don't usually sleep in my apartment and wear my clothes, either," she said, before whining, "Come on, I'm *bored*, and it's not like I can go out on the town in nothing but your t-shirt, can I?"

"What would you do with your father if he was so...portable?"

Morgan barely gave it a second thought before announcing, "Flush him."

"Hmm," I mused, thinking about how that was my first thought, too, back in the day. "A prostitute with daddy issues—how hopelessly cliché."

Morgan flinched at the word, and I remembered then that she hated it. She cleared her throat and tried to move on, which made me feel guilty. I made a mental note to not use that word anymore. "I mean, I wouldn't blame you for hating your father. I looked into your case after the FEEL Center charity benefit."

"Did you?"

"Yes, of course. I had to know what I was getting myself into. All the movies paint you to be some kind of sociopath, you know."

"I noticed," I acknowledged dully. Some part of me wanted to know what she thought, if she thought I was a sociopath, too, but the part of me that trained itself not to care about that sort of thing was stronger.

Morgan revealed, "So, I went straight to the original court documents instead."

"How very pre-law of you."

"Your case was so much more complicated than they made it out to be, I realized," she told me as if I wasn't already aware of this. "It's all so convoluted. Your father's role as a policeman, your age, the obvious abuse, that one blaring detail everyone—*including* your lawyer—seems to gloss over. Side note—I didn't know Dr. Cross was your counsel. She's the one who showed you my website, isn't she? I could get her fired for that, I think."

"You could *try*," I chuckled, knowing my donation practically made Martina damn near impossible to fire for at least the next ten or fifteen years. "What's the blaring detail everyone seems to gloss over?"

"You told everyone you poured the gas all over the house—told on yourself—and yet... You jumped out of a second-story window." Morgan stared at me, letting the dots connect in the silence before stating, "So, your father started the fire before confirming you were safe. They tried you like you were some sort of accomplice." She chuckled and then shook her head. "Idiots."

"And so?" I wanted her to keep going, to see if it was really that obvious to her. I think I wanted it to be, to know there was someone out there who could step away from the situation far enough to ask the right questions. People have a hard time conceptualizing a father callous enough to sacrifice their own. Evidently, Morgan didn't. It made me wonder about her own upbringing. What kind of father did she have to have in order to have such an accurate read on mine?

"He tried to kill you, too, didn't he?" she asked knowingly, but I didn't confirm or deny it. When I didn't say anything, she tilted her head to the side, big eyes sympathetic, lips twisted into a pitying pout. "If I were you, I would've flushed him by now."

Vanilla

Morgan

Almost a full week had passed since Damien had last touched me.

It seemed odd that he would only ask for thirty days of my time and then just let six pass him by without so much as a blowjob. I was beginning to worry. What if I'd been so bad the first time that he was physically repulsed by the thought of touching me again?

The only saving grace was that I was still sleeping in the guest room. And that just five days ago, his assistant showed up with two racks of clothes, which I assumed Damien paid for because while I'd picked up almost everything, I never saw a bill. Surely he wouldn't have bought me clothes if our arrangement was off, right?

Earlier on in the day, I was able to speak to my sister who was under the impression that I had *yet another* new boyfriend I wasn't telling her about.

When it came to Lauren, with the little glimpses she got into my life, she was under the impression that I was her serial dating sister who simply couldn't commit to a man. Despite not doing the boyfriend thing, I let her think whatever she wanted because telling her the truth was a can of worms I refused to open.

All I wanted from my sister was to know if there was ever a time her boyfriend refused to touch her for no discernible reason. It made me cringe to have to ask my sister—one, because she was convinced I had more relationship experience than her, and two, I wasn't even in a relationship with Mr. Fine.

What we had was a... *mutually beneficial agreement.*

Lauren, of course, was no help, because as it turned out, her answer was no. Her perfect fiancé apparently never left her guessing too long.

I was in the kitchen, making myself a cup of that anxiety tea Damien used for sleep late Friday evening. Earlier I had heard the front door shut and I never heard it open again, so I knew the man of the house was out. Perhaps he was out on business. Perhaps giving more money to neglected children. Perhaps on a date. A real date, with a respectable woman who has only had two boyfriends her whole life and only slept with one of them.

Maybe I should've told him I wasn't serious when I said I'd been with hundreds of men. In truth, the count was still higher than the average woman, but it wasn't like I'd slept with any of them. Did he find me disgusting?

Why did I even care?

Almost a week down out of four weeks and I barely had to sleep with him. I should've been celebrating, not worrying.

It was while walking aimlessly between the kitchen and the living room that the sound of the front door shutting startled me to a stop. By the door, Damien was dressed formally, like he'd just returned from some big fancy party.

Or maybe I was right about the date.

Damien looked good in that suit, all black everything over a crisp white dress shirt, matched with a black tie. It reminded me of our fake date night, and how he looked so handsome then, too. He got a haircut since I last saw him; this was obvious from the way his short black hair was cut closer to his scalp, more defined at his hairline. Almost ten feet apart, I could smell him from where I stood. If my nose was correct, he was wearing that expensive vetiver based cologne and—I took a deep breath—peppermint.

Definitely a date.

Just before I could say hello, Damien cut in, "I'm worse for wear tonight, and I'd rather not force the small talk." Translation—*I'm not in the mood; for once shut your talkative ass up*. I pressed my lips together, wondering who pissed in his drink tonight. Wondering if he was going to take it out on me. Wondering if I was going to like it. "Go wait for me in the bathroom—*my* bathroom—and take off the dress. I'll be there in a minute."

I could feel his eyes on me my entire walk across the main space, down the private hallway to the master suite. Damien's bedroom was familiar—because it was similar to the room that I slept in on the opposite side of his apartment. Aside from his bedroom looking a little more lived-in, the main difference was that he had a better view of the city than me. Most of my view was the bay.

Our bathrooms were different, too. While mine was a simple all-white full bath with a single vanity, tub, toilet, and shower, Damien's bathroom was practically a spa. The walls and floors were tiled in giant slabs of white marble, the shower took up an entire wall on its own, a room within its own right where a clawfoot tub sat perched to the side. It felt like the kind of place people might pay to shower.

Just as I was told, I was out of my night gown and alone in Damien's massive bathroom, sitting on the edge of his marble vanity.

At the first sound of his footsteps drawing closer, I hopped off the counter, standing up straight just before he could enter the room. In his hands he held a very large red book and a small glass, half filled with a caramel colored liquor.

The jacket he'd been wearing when he arrived home was off, everything else was left on, even the shoes. I could feel my heart beating in my throat now, watching him get closer. I wanted to ask what the big book was for, but Damien was in dominant mode, so I understood that I wasn't allowed to speak unless spoken to.

And then he was inches away, his eyes going down the length of my body before climbing back up to my eyes. He set his drink down and told me, "Unless

I ask you a question, the only thing I want to hear out of you tonight is your safe word, if you need it."

I swallowed once and he set the book down beside his glass.

Slowly, Damien began unraveling the black belt at his waist. My mind ran wild with theories. Would he hit me with it? Was he going to make me wear it like a leash? Was he just pulling down his pants so that he could pull out his dick? Without the power to ask, I just had to wait and see.

"Hold out your wrists for me." I obeyed, and he soon answered the question in my mind when he wrapped the black belt around both of my wrists, closing it around them very tightly. Damien grabbed the thick book off the bathroom counter, and used the belt to pull me by the wrists into the glass walled shower room. The shower was opulently massive, large enough to comfortably fit six people, with three different types of showerheads along the back marble wall.

Damien placed me underneath the middle one.

On the ground beside my feet, Damien set the book he'd brought in with him down. "Stand on that."

The red book had to have been six inches thick, and standing on it almost made Damien and I the same height. Damien took my bound wrists, raising them above my head and looping the belt around the showerhead pipe twice before buckling it secure. Damien took a step back, openly admiring his bondage handiwork. Even without my saying so, he seemed to know that I wouldn't be able to set myself free even if I tried.

It was uncomfortable, feeling the leather of the belt dig into my skin, but glancing at the book beneath my feet, I knew what was coming.

Wrist suspension is one of the most uncomfortable bondage positions in BDSM—you're robbed of your ability to use your hands, and if your dominant is especially crafty, you'll be far enough off the ground to only stand on your toes. It's not the *worst* pain in the world, but it is painful. You can't kick. If you kick, you'll leave more weight for your wrists to carry, and you could break one.

Or both.

In a moment, Damien would slide that red book from underneath my feet, and I would either have to put all of my weight on my toes, all of my weight on my wrists, or painfully alternate between the two. I waited for him to do it, but instead, he left me standing on the book, alone in the shower room, walking back to the bathroom counter to pick up his drink.

He took a sip of his drink casually, asking, "Is that comfortable?"

I felt like a hanging piece of beef in a butcher shop. "Super."

"That's good. Hold onto that feeling as long as you can." His deep voice was ominous. A coldness pricked at my naked back; goosebumps. Damien began to loosen the black tie around his neck, finishing his drink before re-entering the shower room. I watched as he pulled the loose tie over his head, unraveling the knot once in his hand. As a courtesy, he explained himself before he made any more sudden movements. There was an intoxicating mixture of mint and bourbon on his breath. "I'm going to use this to blindfold you."

And before I could even react, the bathroom went completely pitch black. My breathing quickened, the scent of his cologne coming off the blindfold covered me in an aromatic cloud so thick with spice and bergamot, too, I think.

"You're breathing too fast. It'll make you pass out." The warning sounded experienced. His voice was close. Behind me, I think; I could feel his breath against my neck. He placed one hand on my lower back, warm and slipping to ultimately hold me at my waist. My breathing slowed, a seemingly natural inclination to be comforted by his touch. I wondered if he noticed. I couldn't see his face to see him react.

But I could feel him, the loss of my sight seemed to make every touch feel more provoking. As I suspected it would be, the book underneath my feet was quickly pushed away. Damien's grip on my waist tightened, holding me up to then gradually let me go so that gravity's impact on my arms would be less sudden, preventing any accidental bone fractures.

With nothing to hold me up, most of my weight was pulling down on my bound wrists, with some of the remaining load resting on my two big toes, like some sort of tortured ballerina. Every feeling, good and bad, was amplified by the loss of my eyes.

My senses were in disarray. I could almost taste the cadence of Damien's voice when he spoke again.

"Scale of one to ten—how much pain are you in? Be honest."

The ache was traveling down from my wrists, throbbing at my shoulders and my toes felt like at any moment, they might break. "Seven."

"On a scale of one to ten—how much pain were you in last Saturday?"

When he shoved that disrespectfully big dick into me? "Twenty."

He made a sound of understanding, and without him saying so, I just knew he decided then that seven was a reasonable amount of pain for me to be in.

In the darkness, I felt his hand at my waist slip down, his touch subtly lingering on my behind, before slipping between my legs. Surprised, I took in a sharp breath, and absentmindedly stepped one leg outward to make more room for him. One of his fingers quickly found my clit and he applied just the right amount of pressure, a steady rocking of his hand igniting a spreading heat between my thighs.

There was a momentary pause, and I could feel the heat of Damien's body travel from behind me to directly facing me. Was he still wearing clothes? I couldn't possibly know. Not a moment too soon, his hand returned to my folds, the better angle from the front allowing him to insert one finger into me as he continued to play with my pussy.

And then he inserted a second. I could feel him standing very close, feeling his breath fanning against my lips. So close that if I just pushed my head in a little closer, it would be a kiss. I was sure of it. Even when he spoke, I felt like I was breathing in the sound. "You still feel that seven?"

No.

I actually couldn't.

All I could feel was Damien's hand, his fingers in me, his thumb rubbing rhythmically against my pearl. I shook my head at his question.

"You need to speak when you're spoken to, Morgan," he reminded, intentionally trying to make it harder for me to by increasing his speed. I was so wet that his fingers made a sloshing sound coming in and out of me.

"No, Mr. Fine."

"What's this feel like?" He was goading me.

"Uhh..." I exhaled, so close to climax. "It feels... Mm. It feels... I like it."

"You're about to come, aren't you?"

I nodded, my quickening breaths leaving me unable to speak easily.

There was sincere warning in his tone. "Morgan."

"Yes." I forced the word out, understanding that non-verbal responses were off-limits. "I'm... about to."

And evil as can be, his hand between my thighs slowed to a stop. I could feel my peak descending into nothingness. And without a distraction, pain was back at my wrists, the pressure on them pushing to the forefront of my mind and scaring me into thinking they might snap.

"Say your safe word, if it hurts." Damien was closer to me now, his voice no longer hitting against my lips, but traveling directly into my ear. He wasn't giving me a command as a dominant, he was chipping away at my resolve, trying to take me to a place where I would *want* to say the words. Damien wanted me to *choose* submission, instead of needing to be forced into it.

He wanted me to trust him.

To know that he would stop if I could just be vulnerable enough to tell him I was hurting.

But it felt like losing to me. So instead, I shook my blindfolded head, choosing not to say the words. Even though I wanted to *give* myself to Damien right about now, my pride couldn't allow me to say the safe word out loud.

"I like your spirit, Morgan." His deep, desirous voice made my kitty twitch, and with two fingers in me, I'm sure he felt it. "I really do."

The two fingers slipped out of me and soon his entire hand pulled away. I was left suspended in the darkness, unsure of what was happening now, but from the closeness of his heat, he couldn't have been far. And then his deliciously deep voice emerged again, cutting into the silence to say, "You still taste amazing, by the way."

Even behind a blindfold, I shut my eyes at the sound of that, feeling a shiver travel up my spine. Two fingers were lightly pressed against my lips then, and I recognized my all too familiar scent.

"Here," Damien said. "You try it too. Look how good you taste."

And just like that, he was in my mouth, two warm fingers resting on my tongue. I tried to imagine his face in that moment, wondering which part of my body those dark eyes of his were trained on. Was he breathing steadily? Was he touching himself? Was there a tent in his pants? Was he even wearing pants?

Damien's fingers slipped out of my mouth just as soon as they'd intruded, and for a moment, there was nothing. No touching. No talking. I couldn't even hear him breathing anymore. Did he walk away? The strain on my wrists was growing less tolerable by the minute, and I could feel more of my weight pressing down on my weakened toes. I groaned at the pain, trying to muffle the sound behind sealed lips.

"Hello?" I called out to the darkness, wanting to know if I was alone. No response. What felt like several minutes rolled by, and aside from my own breathing, there was nothing. "Damien?" I used his first name on purpose, knowing he'd immediately correct me if he was in ear shot.

Silence.

What if he was sick enough to leave me here, dangling all night? I tried to shake my head then, rubbing the tightly wrapped blindfold against my raised arm, willing it to slip off my face. The movement aggravated my constraints, and the seven I claimed to feel before immediately jumped to a nine. I cried out then, unable to muffle the sounds this time around. The tie was fastened around my head was secured too well, not budging at all. The word *vanilla* was on the tip of my tongue.

My wrists slipped lower into the constraints and the edge of the belt slid further into my skin, so tight it felt like it might slice through. More impossibly long minutes rolled by. I had no concept of time. Had I been here for twenty minutes? An hour? Two hours? I couldn't tell, but in the time I hung there, the cloth over my eyes had soaked through with both sweat and tears. The belt was cutting into me, I was absolutely sure of it. Pain wise, I was officially at a fifteen, but even worse, I was sure my left wrist was about to snap. My top teeth dug into my lower lip, and I drew in a sharp breath.

"*Van—*"

The belt around my wrists unlatched before I could speak the last two syllables, and just before I could fall to the shower floor, I was caught by two thick, muscled arms. Against my skin, I couldn't feel the fabric of his shirt, so I took that to mean it was off. Damien unraveled the belt around my wrists, and I could feel him inspecting the damage, his thumb passing over an especially tender spot and then immediately pulling back when I flinched.

The moment my wrists were free, my hand immediately went for the blindfold tied around my eyes. He was still holding me when I pushed the necktie down, dragging the loop down around my neck as my breath caught upon finding myself face-to-face with him. Our eyes locked and there was a stillness in the air that felt—for lack of a better word—powerful. *Am I still breathing?*

Damien broke eye contact first, looping and arm behind my knees to lift me up off the ground. We were leaving the bathroom, and as we walked passed the largest mirror in the room, I could see that all he had on was a black pair of boxer briefs. I was grateful that Damien didn't make me walk all the way to the bed; my toes were on fire and it would've been uncomfortable to walk so soon after balancing half my weight on them.

He set me down gently, and I wondered if I still had to be silent. Were we still in dominant-submissive mode? Had he been standing there the whole time while I struggled with the belt constraints? Did he like it? Was he touching himself to the view of me in pain?

I thought he said he'd never been a dominant before. That felt pretty experienced to me.

Damien sat on the edge of the bed where I laid, checking my wrists under the bright light of a bedside lamp. Without a word, he got up and went back into the bathroom. I brought my wrists up to check them myself. Even with my brown complexion, the rubbing of my skin against the belt created significant redness. I had some friction blisters just below the back of my hand. The worst was a visible cut on the outer side of my left wrist; it was bleeding.

Really bad. From the cut, there was a trail of red running down my arm.

I got the feeling that this wasn't supposed to happen.

Maybe he expected me to tap out before things got far enough to draw this much blood.

Out from the bathroom, with a first aid kit in hand, Damien stepped back into the main room and set the opened white box on a bedside table. He didn't say anything to me as he took my wrist back into his hand and set out his materials. Quietly, he dabbed a generous spritz of disinfectant onto the fresh wound before wiping up the excess. I took all of this to mean that we were definitely not in dominant-submissive mode anymore.

"So this is what you do..."

Damien was pulling up an antiseptic ointment packet as he responded, "I'm not sure I know what you mean."

"First you're sour," I explained, feeling him blow on my wrist to dry away the rubbing alcohol. "And then you're sweet. Like a *Sour Patch Kid*. You bend people over tables and then you make them tea. Sour... then sweet."

Damien shook his head, eyebrows coming together amusedly as he fought a smile. He thought my question was amusing, so I must've said something funny, but I didn't know what. "No. I just didn't expect you to damn near dislocate your carpal bone before you safe worded out."

"Is that what you were waiting for? For me to give up?" I asked. He didn't answer that, instead quietly adhering a large bandage to the cut and gently setting my arm back down. I leaned further in, stopping just a few inches shy of his face. "What if I didn't say it? Would you have let me break my wrist."

Damien's brown eyes were on me then, and I don't know why, but I expected his answer to be sentimental. I think some part of me wanted to believe he was a sweet person at heart. Apparently, he wanted nothing more than to quash that belief because he bluntly told me, "I definitely would've let you break your wrist."

The look on my face must've been especially entertaining because he didn't bother reeling in his laugh. The sound of it warmed my insides, but I tried not to notice. I didn't know if he was joking, and I'm not sure I'll ever really know.

"Lay your head back, Morgan," he doled out the order calmly.

It wasn't over, I realized, letting my back fall against his thick and fluffy white pillows. I watched as he moved from my side, down to the end of the bed. Damien hand eased between my naked thighs, dividing my legs for a full on view of my kitty and my breath picked up.

"Is this..." I gasped at the first touch of his tongue, pressing the back of my head further into the pillow behind me. As a reflex, because I couldn't touch him, I pushed my up my hips as if to hold myself closer to his mouth. "...your idea of an apology?"

Not that I was complaining.

Only briefly, he pulled back to ask, "What exactly would I be apologizing for?"

"You left... me... hanging... in the bathroom... for so... long." It was difficult to speak as he waged an assault on my most sensitive parts, his warm tongue slipping in and out of me before climbing up to my pulsating clit. One of Damien's hands came up to hold me down at my stomach, keeping me pressed against the mattress with legs opened wide, and with his free hand, he pushed two fingers in as his tongue continued to draw low moans from deep within me.

Just as I was beginning to feel that telltale heat hit its peak, Damien pulled back again if only just to drive me nuts. "Who says I left?" he asked.

And then he was back, genuinely trying to multi-task this conversation and driving me completely crazy.

"So... you... didn't... hear... ahh—" I grabbed an extra pillow beside my head and brought it up to press my face into it, trying to quiet my moans. Damien's steadying hand at my stomach grabbed onto one corner of the pillow, snatched it away, and tossed it off the bed where I couldn't reach it; clearly he wanted me to get loud. "You could hear... uhh... me call... calling for you?"

From between my legs, I could feel him nodding his response. The speed of his tongue was rhythmic and lustful. Most men eat pussy like it's a chore, and some men do it like it's just as fun for them as it is for you. Damien was definitely the latter. My moans were getting louder, and I was losing control of the way my hips bucked to meet the motions of his mouth, each of my little reactions seemingly making him go harder, making him come on more strongly. He pushed a third finger into me, the pumping of his hand just as dedicated as his tongue.

"Then why didn't... didn't you help... me?"

"Because you were still playing that power game," he whispered against me. "Be vulnerable, Morgan. That means if I hurt you—if you're at a twenty out of ten—you tell me in that moment. You safe word out. Don't hold out, thinking you're power tripping, because you're not. Don't hurt yourself trying to convince yourself that taking on unnecessary pain means you're strong. You're a submissive right now. Start acting like it."

His tongue—thank God—was back on me then, the surprise of the reunion casting a whimpering cry out of me, that final touch being just what I needed to send me completely over the edge and toward climax, held between his hands as my body quaked with the waves. As I came down from that high, I managed to squeak out, "Is that why you haven't touched me all week? Because you were mad at me for letting you hurt me? Because I've been a bad submissive?"

There was a pause, his eyes rising from between my thighs to meet my eyes, and his answer was simple.

"I was giving you time to recover." *Oh.* "Because believe it or not, I don't get off on hurting you. Remember—sadism is your thing, not mine. But if you let yourself get hurt because you're too stubborn to be just a little bit vulnerable—I will not stop you."

"And if I'm vulnerable?"

With earnest, easy to believe brown eyes, he promised, "Then I will never hurt you."

DON'T MAKE IT WEIRD

MORGAN

Damien's arm was wrapped around me tightly when I woke the next morning

We were together in his bed, me still naked from the night before, and I could feel the fabric of his boxers pressing onto my behind. That scent of cologne was still on his skin, but it was subtle now, like I wouldn't even smell it if I didn't already know what he was supposed to smell like.

In all my girlish fantasies about life and love, this was exactly how I wanted to be held by my lover. It was a possessive touch, the way his arm snaked around my waist and hand rested on upper thigh, big spooning me close, just screamed—*mine*.

And in my fantasies, it was unclear who was owned exactly. Me, for letting him hold me this way, or him, for needing to hold me this close.

I rolled slowly on his arm, finding behind me his eyes still shut, still deep asleep. I took this moment to study him—his chocolate brown skin, flawlessly unmarked and smooth, thick black brows over his closed eyes, and eyelashes long enough to touch the tops of his cheeks.

He was beautiful this way, and I wondered how many women before me had this memory saved. It wasn't lost on me that these types of curiosities were not normal for a submissive to express. I wasn't supposed to care if he had one or one thousand women. We weren't together. According to him, we weren't even equals.

Damien stirred a little, as though feeling me staring at him now. He looked younger when he was asleep, that ever-present discerning crease between his brows smoothed out and made him look more carefree.

"How long have you been staring at me?"

Damien's sudden voice made my back go straight; his eyes were still closed. How long had he been awake, watching me watch him?

"I wasn't keeping time," I answered, watching his eyes open to an inquisitively raised eyebrow. "You're very *cute* when you sleep."

He grimaced at this, his arm around my waist loosening and then completely unraveling itself from around me.

"You were awake for how long?"

"From the moment you rolled around on my arm," he replied. "Which hurt, by the way."

I pulled up my bandaged left wrist. "Well, so did this."

He frowned. "All you had to do was tap out."

"So, is that your thing?" I wondered, staring into his eyes, trying to ignore the intimacy of this set up. In his bed, not a stitch of clothing on my body, shining under the morning sun—this was practically pillow talk. "Making me beg for mercy? You get off on that?"

His hand was back at my waist, pulling me in closer, the suddenness of it all making my heart stutter in my chest. "I like not having to compete for the upper hand every waking moment."

I felt my right cheek lift with a smile. "Now, where's the fun in that?"

It was easy to see that desire in his eyes, and I briefly wondered if the second time would hurt less. A little part of me was curious, even. That didn't negate the fact that curiosity killed the cat, and *that* dick... was quite likely to be the death of *my* kitty for a second time.

Damien's second hand pressed into the mattress beside me, his body rose above mine, and there was a pause. I could feel his other hand warm against my waist, holding me in such a way that didn't feel self-serving at all. So, unlike a dominant, his hand on me was a comforting touch. Underneath the shade of his shadow, my eyes rose to meet his hovering above, and I could've sworn he stopped breathing.

We stopped breathing.

Damien took the first breath, breaking me out of that seconds-long trance. Neither of us had acknowledged the eerie stillness, both of us acting as if we hadn't noticed it. When I felt him press against my opening, it was like time began acting normal again, if not sped up. I rushed to fill my lungs, grabbing a fistful of the white sheets underneath. But he didn't move too quickly.

I could still feel him paused against me. Damien was rock hard, warm against my outer folds, just kind of coasting the border of my insides. He wasn't quite in me, but he was in far enough for the outer lips of me to kiss the stony head of him. We were suspended in that in-betweenness for a while, just letting my natural juices coat him. I liked it, the gentleness of it all. It was bizarrely intimate.

His deep voice vibrated through his body and against my clit when he spoke. "You'll tell me if I'm hurting you?"

That first night with Damien, through the pain—in spite of everything—he did bring me to climax. Twice.

I hated it.

And I loved it.

Of course, the next morning, I felt it all rushing back to me with none of the orgasmic warmth to cushion the sting, but I couldn't tell myself lies when I found myself, days later, craving him again. Pain and fear be damned. I wanted this. I wanted him.

Pain can be arousing sometimes. Among the normies, masochism gets such a bad rap. What they don't understand is that in the mind, pain and euphoria are separated by a very fine line, and if done with expert precision, these two feelings may be felt in a complementary way. This kind of stimulation is confusing for many, but when done just right, the payoff is simply...

Those orgasms can be life changing.

"I'll tell you," I whispered. A lie. A little part of me wanted it to hurt. Wanted the bad to mix with the good so that I may never forget what this was. He was not my boyfriend. We were not a couple. We were not making love.

This was a mutually beneficial agreement. A business transaction.

He filled every last inch of me, eyes in mine the way a dominant's eyes never linger on a submissive, and I understood why Damien wanted me at a distance. I understood why he needed boundaries. How easy it would be for me *own* him if we were equals in this bed.

I could see it now, feeding back from his brown eyes, that willingness to give me whatever I desired so long as I could wrap my body around him like this and humble myself long enough to ask for it. He could be mine, I realized in the light of the day.

And he knew it, too.

The fit was tight, and I only realized now how aroused I was because the slip of him was easier now than it was the first time—and I had been incredibly wet the first time, too. I couldn't keep looking into his eyes. It was doing concerning things the regularity of my heartbeat. I brought up a hand, wrapping around to the back of his neck to pull him down, bringing the side of his face to the side of mine, our cheeks pressed together.

This is not how subs touch their doms during sex...

"You were in a bad mood last night." My whispered words chased away the thoughts swirling in my head, trying to ignore the slippery slope I was on. *This is too intimate...* In his ear, I continued, "But you were dressed nice. Was it a bad date?"

His first thrusts were slow. For my sake, I determined, closing my eyes to the delectably gentle friction of his body inside of mine. Where was the pain? It felt so comforting, like it was all for me. *This is too sweet...* His rich baritone emerged, "You sound a little bit jealous."

"I *am* jealous." I moaned the words, breathing slow exhales against his neck as my hardened nipples rubbed against his naked chest. He held one hand on my waist and the other at the middle of my back. "You get to sleep with as many women as you want, and when it comes to men, I just get one. I hate that for me."

Damien's next movement within me was harder, a punishing thrust that hit me at the ends of my insides and made my stomach plunge. He was displeased with what I said, showing me then that he could make this hurt if he wanted to. A cross between a quiet scream and moan drew out of me and I made sure it hit him right in his ear.

It made me smile when his grip at my waist tightened, drawing me closer to him as if to hold me through the wave that washed through me. A soothing touch, but everything hurt so good.

"You're always so serious, Mr. Fine," I chided when all had calmed. "Have a sense of humor."

"Be funny," Damien whispered back. He revealed to me then, "I wasn't on a date."

"Why were you—" He pushed into me again, expertly measuring out just the right amount of speed necessary, to cut me off into a gasp before I finished my question. "—so sour then?"

"Event for the last day... of FEEL Charity Week," he spoke in fragmented sentences, speed steadily increasing as he dipped in and out of me, his own breath picking up. "Bad run in with... the local media."

"Oh, are you alr—"

"We don't have to talk about it, Morgan." *God, please keep saying my name while you hold me like this.* He rose up from my ear to meet my eyes, his rhythmic pushes and pulls beat music into my stomach, and opened myself up to him complete. *Take me. Take me as rough and as quick as you like*, I communicated to him with my eyes as he added, "We don't have to talk at all."

But I wanted us to talk about it. I wanted him to be a little bit vulnerable about his troubles with me. I didn't want to be some sex object he could channel his frustrations into. I wanted to be someone he could confide in instead—a friend.

"Don't make it weird by catching feelings," he whispered then, as if he could see my desire to be his friend swimming around in my eyes. "Stop looking at me like that."

It made me self-conscious, not knowing how I was looking at him in that moment, not knowing what kind of secrets my eyes were telling. Was it even friendship that I wanted? What if my eyes told him I wanted more than that? The unknown of it all made me crave the upper hand.

My eyes were off him in seconds. I wrapped my legs around Damien and pulled to the side so that we might switch places, and then he was underneath me, watching me from bellow with hazed over eyes that felt hotter than the shining sun on my body. Submissives don't get to be on top unless told to get on top. Damien either didn't know or he didn't care.

I sat across his hips, feeling him nestled deep within every available crevice in me and for a moment, I felt like Mistress Morgan again—with a man at my mercy. I always felt safest—most secure—when I could dominate. I could pretend better from this angle, ride him to completion at a pace that I set—get him off quickly before he saw anything else in my eyes.

Damien pulled me down to him, holding me closer as his hips bucked to meet each bounce. And I could feel his lips against my hair, breathing warm against me as we quickened pace faster and faster until a growling breath lifted up from his chest. I felt the heat of him grow fuller and warmer inside of me and we came together, like we shared a body in that moment.

When I pulled back, his eyes on me were hot, radiating a silent plea to not move.

Not now. Not ever.

And then I understood what he must've saw in my eyes. He saw how much I wanted this moment to mean more than a simple business transaction. And right then, I could see that same desire in his own eyes.

Damien

I didn't ask for enough time.

With her, thirty days might past like thirty seconds, and had I known it would be like this, I would've asked for a year at least. Morgan and I were on day twenty-three, the end of the third week, and I had never been more conscious of how many days were in a week than now.

The past couple of weeks had been enjoyable. Morgan spent more time in my bed than her own as of late, but we liked it that way. Every day she felt less and less like a transactional companion and more like a genuine friend. She was a lot smarter than I initially gave her credit for.

Seven more days and she would be free to leave.

I should've asked for more time.

It was late in the evening. Morgan was seated across the dining room table, a wine glass filled with water in her hand. When she was nineteen, she'd gotten drunk at a party she'd dragged her sister to, and her sister was assaulted. Morgan hadn't touched alcohol since.

I'd learned this about her some time last week, tangled in the sheets of my bed, when I asked her why she didn't drink. Like I'd asked her to be days before, she was vulnerable with me, expressing her never-ending guilt despite her sister's forgiveness. Morgan refused to drink as a form of atonement. So that she might never forget what happened.

For dinner tonight, Morgan said she made one of the three dishes she made well, and evidently one of them was lasagna. It sat at the center of the table, steaming from melted cheese and red sauce.

"This looks good." *You look good*, I felt like I should say instead. She was pretty tonight, effortlessly. The bangs of her pixie cut were pinned back and away from her forehead, revealing the flawless brown skin underneath. When she smiled in response to my praise, her dimples sunk into her cheeks the same way they would sink into her cheeks when she had her lips wrapped around my—

There was a knock at the front door, which was odd for this time of day. Usually a knock earlier in the day meant that Chloe was stopping by with some documents from work or more clothes for Morgan who never seemed to wear the same outfit twice. It was obvious that while her clothing was being bought on my dime, she was taking full advantage. It didn't bother me.

But it was too late in the day for work or new clothes.

The knock sounded again, harder the second time before the calling started. "Damien, open up!"

I sighed, recognizing the voice, wondering if the desperation in his tone meant it had been ages since his last high, debating whether I should send the girl across from me at the table to her room before letting him in. That entitledness about him got the better of Sebastien and he was beating down my door now.

To Morgan's slightly frightened features I assured, "Relax. It's just my brother."

STOCKHOLM SYNDROME

DAMIEN

It had been close to a month since I'd last seen Sebastien.

Sometime two weeks ago, I'd sent him a bank transfer and from the looks of him now, he'd burned through that money quick. Even with the tattooed sleeves, it was easy to spot the red dots along his arms, signs of recent injections. I checked my brother's eyes for dilated pupils, fully ready to slam the door in his face if he had the audacity to show up at my place strung-out yet again.

Sebastien stood at the threshold, an almost mirror image of my own face. From what I could see, he was sober. "You having dinner? It smells good."

The bones on Sebastien's wrists were protruding and defined. Somehow, he'd gotten thinner since I'd last seen him. How thin he was always mad my stomach twist. Even Morgan had more meat on her bones than he did. I stepped to the side and nodded him in. He should eat something.

"Who's this?" I didn't have to turn away from the front door to know that Sebastien would be standing at the center of the foyer, eyes trained on my dinner guest, hands stuffed in his pockets. Sebastien always rethought his approach to asking for money whenever there was a pretty woman present.

He was shameless, but he wasn't *that* shameless. It still embarrassed him to act like a beggar in front of the right people. In the past, I could recall my little brother switching up in front of girlfriends and companions like Morgan. He'd leave and then they'd shoot me a look, if I'd ever complained about him, and just say, '*He's not that bad.*'

Little did they know. He'd be back at a later date, hoping they wouldn't be here, to try asking for money again. Morgan didn't know it—but she'd just saved me a couple thousand dollars this evening by simply looking pretty.

"You must be his brother," she guessed from her seat at the table.

"He told you about me?" Sebastien sounded wary, like he feared I might've told the truth about him to a cute girl he'd just met. *Couldn't have that, could we?*

Morgan shook her head. "No. You just look exactly like him, and you're way too old to be his son."

Sebastien looked at me then, searching for his own face in mine before shaking his dreads.

"Nah, I don't see it," he announced and then asked me, "Can I stay for dinner, Dame?"

I looked at Morgan, pushing up my eyebrows as if to tell her it was her call to make, and then as an afterthought, I remembered that she was playing submissive. By all intents and purposes, I wasn't supposed to be asking her if my own brother could sit at my dinner table and eat food I paid for. Whether or not she was uncomfortable with it wasn't supposed to be relevant to me, but for the past few days, Morgan had been feeling less and less like a submissive and more like a friend.

"We have enough," she told me, thinking that must've been the question I was asking.

Sebastien didn't waste any time, taking the adjacent seat to Morgan's as I went to get him a plate from the kitchen. "You're a little young for Damien. What are you, twenty-two?"

"Twenty-three," she corrected and then shrugged, telling him, "And I've been with older."

I wished Morgan hadn't been so honest with him. Not because I found it particularly bothersome that there had been people with her before me. Truthfully—I *didn't* care. I knew who she was when I asked for a month of her time. The reason why I'd wished she'd been a little demurer was because Sebastien wasn't stupid. He could hear a statement like that and catch the multiple different meanings it could take on.

His eyes cut across the room to me, and quickly bounced back to her, an idea formulating behind that squinted gaze of his. Sebastien had a hypothesis in his eyes, and from the way he smiled at me knowingly, I would venture to say he knew. I took my seat across from Morgan, setting Sebastien's plate in front of him, my eyes daring him to step an inch out of line. *Act like you've got some fucking sense*, I conveyed the message with my expression alone.

"This looks good." He gestured to the pasta dish at the center of the table. "You made this?"

Morgan nodded modestly, reaching for the serving spatula to cut me a piece before serving herself.

"Oh, and she fixes your plate before she fixes hers," my brother noted before serving himself. This was something I also couldn't ignore because it was out of character for Morgan. Of the dozen times we'd shared a meal together these past few weeks, being served was something new.

"This is not bad," Sebastien acknowledged after the first bite, amusing himself by adding, "for a prostitute."

Morgan's fork dropped onto her plate.

"I'm *not* a prostitute," she automatically corrected him. She must've assumed I had told him that because she briefly glanced at me and glared. Even though I hadn't used that word in weeks, I'd called her that enough times for her to assume my brother's assumptions were coming from something I'd said. She held her head high, starting to explain, "What Mr. Fine and I have is a—"

"Morgan," I cut her off before she could say more than she needed to. "Don't engage."

She pressed her lips together, taking that as an order from her dominant rather than a warning born out of general concern from a friend. *Don't argue with my brother*, I should've told her. *He isn't worth it.*

"She's obedient." Sebastien chuckled and I could see Morgan visibly cringe from her end of the table. Gone was the version of my brother putting on airs for the pretty girl. He'd taken in her age and her *'I've been with older'* comment and immediately guessed she was being paid in some way to be here. Like I said, Sebastien wasn't stupid. "If you don't mind sharing—would she listen to you if you told her to play with me tonight?"

But he *had* lost his damn mind.

Morgan's head snapped in his direction and when she looked at me, her eyes were wide with anxiety, as if she wasn't sure what my only answer could be. Of course, I'd never share her with my brother, but one look at her and it was clear she didn't know that. Part of me wondered where the spitfire I'd met almost a month ago was; the girl who barged into my office and made her demands would've cursed Sebastien clean out by now. What had changed?

"May I be excused from the table?" Her voice was small; smaller than I'd ever heard it. When I nodded, her movements were immediate, leaving her food at the table untouched and headed straight for the hallway that led to her bedroom. Sebastien continued to eat, unbothered by the fact that he'd made her so uncomfortable that she felt the need to leave. Just before Morgan could head down the hall, she stopped by the small bar I kept off the edge of the living room and tucked a full bottle under her arm.

"Get up." The anger in my tone threw Sebastien off guard, his fork stopping midway to his mouth before he set it back down to question me with his eyes.

"What'd I do?"

It pissed me off that he would even ask. "Get up."

And he rose, leaving a half-eaten dinner on his plate and I ushered him further and further out of the dining room, until we were at the front door again. Sebastien scoffed at the realization that he was being kicked out—as if Morgan wasn't worth this response.

"The fuck is your problem, huh?" I asked him when we were out in the private hallway just outside the penthouse.

"What?" Sebastien matched my volume, as if hoping for the sound to travel and find its way back to Morgan. "What's the big deal? You really in my face over some hoe you picked up off the—"

My fist collided with the left side of Sebastien's jaw, cutting him off mid-sentence. I couldn't remember the last time I'd hit him like this, but he was practically begging for it tonight. "Watch the shit you say about her in front of me."

"What is she—*my* age?" Sebastien questioned before spitting the blood collecting in his mouth onto the hallway's white tile floor. "If you wanted to punch me for whatever sadistic reason, you don't have to hide behind her to do it. I'm supposed to buy that you have this deep-rooted affection for some bitch fresh out of—"

The second punch shut him up. Sebastien cradled his face, taking several paces backward, feeling safe enough to talk his shit as he continued to create space. "I'm not coming around here *anymore*—" An obvious lie. He'd be back. "—and fuck you, Damien!"

I knocked twice before letting myself into Morgan's bedroom. She was seated against the black headboard, her knees pulled up to her chest and balancing a half-full bottle of 15-year-old *Macallan*. Her eyes were red when she looked up from the bottle and at me.

"Did you drink all of that?" I questioned, and she simply shrugged, barely reacting when I took the empty seat beside her. "I thought you didn't drink."

"I don't," she assured, her words already sounding a little slurred. I took the bottle from her knees, tightening the metal cap around the mouth. "I just don't want to touch your brother," she told me then, as if I would ever consider making her. "Don't make me."

Was she getting herself drunk in preparation for—?

"I would never ask you to do something like that."

"You like control," she told me. "You're not very good at being a dominant in the BDSM sense, but the one thing you keep consistent with all dominants is that need for control."

"I wouldn't exercise control over you to the point of making you have sex with someone you don't want to—"

"You make me have sex... have sex with *you*, don't you?" she cut me off, drunkenly stumbling over her words. "Do you think because you make me cum that it's not wrong? You hold Stanford over my head and bend me to compliance, and I'm supposed to think a stand-up guy like yourself wouldn't share me if asked nicely? Maybe you said no because you respect me," she muttered. "Or maybe you just don't like to share your toys."

"Morgan—"

"No... I have to tell you something before you try and shut me up again. Something you need to hear so you can understand what you did—what you've done. I'm getting comfortable, Mr. Fine. I'm acclimating to this role you've put me in, sleeping in your bed, making you dinner. I thought I was falling in love with you until tonight. It's Stockholm Syndrome, maybe.

"Tonight was a wake up call. It reminded me of why I was the way that I was, and I'm tired of pretending like being your submissive isn't triggering the fuck out of me every other day." She sighed, letting that liquid courage course through her veins. "When I was seventeen—my father gave me to his best friend, and his best friend raped me. And I'm going to tell you the story."

Mayor Jean-Baptiste

Morgan

When I was in my junior year of high school, the mayor came to our house for dinner. It wasn't supposed to be a big deal because only three months earlier, he had only been mayoral *candidate* Herschel Jean-Baptiste, our dad's best friend. That evening, however, Mom and Dad rolled out the red carpet for a man who had been in our house at least a thousand times before.

Mayor Jean-Baptiste was Miami's first ever black mayor. He was a member of the all-black country club my parents were members of, and everyone in the club was very proud that one of our own was leading the city.

That December, just before my sister and I turned seventeen, he came to dinner and in the middle of the meal, announced that he was in need of an intern up at the mayor's office, and he couldn't think of a better candidate besides... *Lauren.*

Lauren was always Daddy's favorite.

She was pretty, she was smart, well-mannered—perfect in our father's eyes. Lauren was in the room, and it was like Daddy forgot he had a second daughter. In those early years, I nearly drove myself crazy trying to win him over. I tried to have the best grades. I took up tennis because I knew Daddy liked tennis, and Lauren wasn't good at it. I even tried to make myself prettier than my identical twin somehow.

Of course, all of Daddy's friends loved Lauren; he'd bragged about her enough times for everyone to know she was the special twin. But that evening, Daddy took an opportunity from his golden child and blessed me with it.

"Morgan doesn't have any internships on her college applications," he'd said over dinner, as if imploring the new mayor to take pity on his less impressive offspring. "Why doesn't she intern for you instead?"

It was the first time in recent memory that I could recall my father getting me something without my asking. Across the dinner table, Mayor Jean-Baptiste had eyed me carefully at first and then ultimately nodded, concluding, "I'm sure she'll do great."

I was ecstatic. It was a way to prove myself. Mayor Jean-Baptiste was my father's closest friend and if he grew to appreciate me, maybe that might rub off on my ever-neglectful father. Maybe he'd see me as capable and worthy for once.

That was how I found myself working four hours a day at the mayor's office over winter break. The building was in transition mode following the election, with the new mayor bringing in new faces daily. As an intern, I was meant to pick up coffee orders, run back and forth from the copy machine, and on occasion, they'd have me handling the receptionist's desk, too.

Mayor Jean-Baptiste had promised to write me a letter of recommendation for my college applications, and things were going smoothly. Although, we'd made to my last day interning and no letter had been written.

We were in the first week of January on my last day as an intern. I was sitting at my little makeshift desk just outside of the mayor's office when Mayor Jean-Baptiste came into work from the rain. He seemed to be in a rotten mood on account of getting drenched without an umbrella, but it was my last opportunity to remind him about that letter of recommendation.

Later that afternoon, I had tennis practice, so I was dressed in my usual tennis skirt and white polo shirt. It hadn't been the first time I had worn my tennis uniform to the office, but that day, I felt especially naked when Mayor Jean-Baptiste's eyes slid down the length of my legs and then back up to my face.

He licked his lips. "Yes, of course."

At the time, I felt something in my stomach churn with nausea. Mayor Jean-Baptiste was older than my father and he was giving me the eyes—that look I would go on to recognize as lust when I wizened up. Unfortunately for me then, on that day, I was still too naive.

Damien

"He called me into his office about half an hour before my dad was due to pick me up from work," Morgan continued to tell her story, though from what she'd said before, I already knew the ending.

"His office was... pristine. Not a single crooked picture frame on the wall. His desk—spotless. I hate being in offices like that—the ones that feel like they're for show and not for work. Mayor Jean-Baptiste had an office like that. Sometimes when I go to sleep, I can still see my reflection on the dark wood of his tabletop."

I recalled something she said weeks ago that I hadn't understood at the time—*I love messy desks. They make me feel safe somehow.*

Morgan continued to tell her story, "He was standing by the door when I came in. '*Your letter is on the desk,*' he said. I went to go get it and he slid up behind me. '*Read it,*' he said, breathing down the back of my neck. He smelled like the rain, and to this day, I hate the smell.

"I was young—I was only seventeen. I froze up, understanding that something weird was taking place, but no more assertive enough to face it confrontationally. And he was already in such a bad mood. I thought if I ignored how weird he was being, he might stop. In hindsight, ignoring it might've encouraged him. His hands were on my shoulders then, pushing me over the desk until my cheek pressed hard into the wood surface.

"The mayor's hands were up my skirt, hiking up the hem, and I cried. I said no. I had a panic attack right then as it happened, but I couldn't scream. I could barely breathe. The rec letter in my hand crumpled—I never got a chance to read it. When he was finished with me, he pulled back and saw the blood on his skin, and said, 'Good heavens, were you a virgin?' Like he hadn't expected that of me... Like he couldn't believe his luck."

The first night she was here...

Oh fuck, the table.

She was having a panic attack, and I made light of the situation. I was starting to feel sick. She was having a fucking panic attack and instead of taking a step back from it all and simply asking her what was wrong, I let my prejudice control my response. She was a girl with a lingerie-clad booking site, and I treated her as nothing more than that.

When she started crying that night, I should have stopped, but I didn't.

People have made wild assumptions about me and my character all my life, but I have never felt more like a monster than I did right now.

"I told my dad," she whispered, wiping her cheeks quickly before I could see her tears. "He didn't call the police. He didn't talk to him. My father said he didn't *believe* me. He made me promise I wouldn't tell anyone else. How disgraceful it would've been for my father if his daughter's lies ruined the career of Miami's first black mayor." Morgan couldn't hold back the sob that erupted from her then. "But sometimes... I think he knows. You can't be friends with someone for as long as he was friends with the mayor and not know what they're capable of." She wrapped her arms around herself, bringing her knees closer to her chest. "And that's why Mayor Jean-Baptiste couldn't have Lauren."

"I hate it when men touch me," Morgan confessed, finally looking at me for the first time since she started telling this story. "That's why I was a dominatrix—because that way, everything happens on my terms. Not here, though. I hate how powerless being here makes me feel." She wiped her face again, erasing all sign of shed tears. "I tried to convince myself that I could like it. I made a list of reasons why this month was a worthy sacrifice, but... Being powerless in the presence of a man terrifies me. It will always *terrify* me."

Morgan

For the first time in weeks, I woke up alone.

At first, it was disorienting, reaching toward the other side of the bed, and feeling nothing but the tangle of bedsheets. *Where is Damien?* I thought to myself before the recap of last night's confessional came flooding back through my morning-after, booze-fueled haze.

In an instant, I was seated upright against the headboard, wondering what that unsolicited episode of honesty might've costed me. Almost five years of sobriety down the drain, and who knows what else I might've lost in the process. What if I said too much?

There were no sounds coming from the outside of my room. No bubbling coffeemaker. No running water at the sink. No sounds of the morning financial report in the living room. This was my first sign that something was off, because by this hour, Damien was usually getting his morning started.

When I stepped out of my bedroom, and into the living space, I immediately felt like something had been changed. It was only after staring into the dining room for three minutes straight that my hungover, sleepy brain realized that the dining room table was gone.

Weird, I thought, walking further into the kitchen to find a note on the refrigerator that hadn't been there last night. On a plain white sheet of paper, in Damien's handwriting, was a short note.

I am personally handling your Stanford rejection appeal.

Expect a letter by the end of the week.

You can go home now.

I'm sorry.

VOICEMAILS

MORGAN

In the days following my return to my apartment, I thought about him more than I would've cared to admit. He used me; literally blackmailed me into submission, and there I found myself at the randomest of moments—thinking about him.

It had never been in my nature to be swayed by simple '*I'm sorrys*', but for Damien, some part of me wanted to make an exception. The compulsion was always strongest at night, lying awake in my bed, remembering what it felt like to have my naked skin pressed against his warmth. He tried not to make it obvious, but he liked me there just as much as I liked being there, but then again, I tried to not make it obvious as well.

Did he think I hated all of it? I couldn't be sure. It should have been obvious that I didn't. Sometimes, I think it was pretty damn obvious that I liked him. Especially in those moments, when he would seemingly forget the power dynamics he'd set. I could just be Morgan and he was just Damien.

I'd never had that before, a person—a man—I could just curl into and sleep with. No dominatrix facades to keep up, no bitten tongues of a silent submissive Morgan. I could just sleep, feeling his arm twist around my waist and feel safer for it. That, I liked.

I'd never given much thought to how cold the bed feels when you're the only one in it.

I missed him.

Maybe just a little.

My time following the return back to my apartment carried on slow and mostly uneventful. The Mistress Morgan website remained closed, for fear of undoing whatever magic Damien was doing for me behind the scenes. I spent my evenings packaging bundles for the few hair customers I had. It certainly wasn't dominatrix money, but it was enough to cover my bills without having to dip into my savings.

It was on a Friday, the day that would've been my last Friday with Damien, when a thick envelope arrived in my mailbox from Stanford, California. I was in my tiny dining room, ripping at the sealed paper with shaking hands, breathing quickening as I unraveled the tri-folded sheets of paper out to the word:

Congratulations.

It felt like a two-ton weight that I'd been carrying for months had finally slid its way down my shoulders. Congratulations. Finally—a congratulations.

After careful review of your appeal, the admission committee would like to formally grant...

I felt as if I should call him. There weren't many people I could celebrate with. Everyone I knew would want to know how my appeal was pushed through so quickly. I stared at my cell phone for twenty minutes before I finally caved.

It rang three times.

"Your call has been forwarded to an automatic voice message system."

"Hey, it's me, Morgan." I was pacing in my apartment's kitchen. Around me, there were boxes of my belongings, half-filled and labeled for Palo Alto. "You probably already know this, but I got my acceptance letter two months ago, and I've been meaning to call, but every time I do, it goes to voicemail, so I'm finally just leaving a message. We finished off on a very awkward spot, and I think it would be good for both of us if we could have some sort of heart-to-heart. Anyways—call me back when you get this message."

"Hey, it's me, Morgan. Again." I was pacing around an empty studio apartment in Palo Alto. The small space smelled of fresh paint and new carpet. "Just moved to the Bay Area, and I was thinking about... you... today. I don't know. This is stupid—you won't even return my calls. Look, about that night—I was just triggered by the thought of you sharing... When I told you that story, I wasn't implying that you..." I stopped talking, unable to find the right thing to say in a one-minute voicemail. There was just too much to say. "I wish we could talk about this."

"I'm sorry, too," I spoke into the receiver. It was late in California, so I knew it was even later where Damien was. "You took advantage of my desperation, but if I could do it all over, I'd still let you. Yes—because I wanted to get into Stanford, but also because... because I was curious about you. I shouldn't have guilt tripped you the way that I did. Being your submissive wasn't that bad. Compared to me, you were practically a feminist as a dominant. I didn't—I didn't hate it."

"Tomorrow's my 1L Orientation." I sighed, telling myself that this would be my last voicemail. "I can't believe it's really happening, and it dawned on me today that I never said thank you. You're probably not going to return this call either, but you haven't changed your number yet, so I'm assuming you're listening to these messages. Remember when you said that if I was vulnerable, you would never hurt me? This is me being vulnerable—I miss you. And it hurts me that you won't talk to me."

1L Orientation was a two-day experience held on Stanford's law campus to welcome the incoming first year law students. It was normal to be anxious on a day like today, meeting all my future classmates and professors. My stomach had been doing back-flips for the past thirty-six hours.

On the second day, like everyone else, I was dressed in a pair of slacks and a crisp white dress shirt. In the past few months since getting my acceptance letter, my hair had grown out enough for me to pull off a half up, half down hairstyle. I thought I looked nice. Modest, even.

Forty first years were gathered in a lecture hall on the south end of campus, getting the rundown from one of many professors on what was to be expected from us this year. Late policies. Exam protocol. Textbook and supply requirements. Et cetera, et cetera.

I was seated at the front of the class, taking notes on important details so's to not forget anything. Law school would be different from undergrad, every professor kept reiterating. Already, I had met three or four classmates who were forming future study groups, all inviting me to join. When the last professor began to wrap up his introductory speech, he made way for the final speaker, Dr. Martina A. Cross.

She was just as pretty as I remembered her—flawless almond brown skin and pin straight black hair, cut in a razor-sharp straight line at her shoulders. She greeted the room with a radiant smile—the corners of her maroon-painted mouth free from residue this time around.

"Welcome to Stanford." Her smile was beaming as she scanned the room, and when her eyes landed on me, her expression fell. "My name is Dr. Cross and I will be your Dean of Admissions & Financial Aid this year. We at the office of financial aid have an exciting announcement. This year is especially exciting because due to a large donation made to our school by a generous donor, the aid office is granting full tuition to the students in the top-ten percent of their class by the end of their first semester.

"Your incoming class is made up of one-hundred and six students, so that means that by the end of the semester, ten of you will be selected as Fine Scholars. From there you can expect your full tuition and living expenses to be covered by the fund for the duration of your law school experience. We know how difficult it can be to get scholarships in professional programs, and we have decided this is the fairest method of ensuring an even playing field for all students."

People around the room let out cheers at the thought of competing for a top ten spot. Dr. Cross went down a laundry list of other resources available to students at the financial aid office and soon dismissed the buzzing freshman to head to their next orientation session.

"Miss Caplan." I heard my name being called as I gathered my things, looking up to find Dr. Cross standing closer to my table now. "May I have a word?"

She waited until the entire room had cleared out before she spoke again, looking slightly down at me from the bottoms of her eyes as she stood in six-inch heels that had her towering a good three inches above my head.

"You seem quite pleased to have whored yourself out for a seat a the table."

I stuttered. "I—I'm sorry, I'm not sure I know what you—"

"Is that how you solve all your problems?" Dr. Cross wondered, stepping closer to me. "On your back?"

My whole body cringed. "Dr. Cross—"

"Don't even try it. You wouldn't expect me to believe Damien Fine went over my head, and personally contacted the school's Dean about your application out of the kindness of his own heart, would you?" Dr. Cross shook her head. "I can't imagine you feel like you've truly *earned* your spot. Do you?"

"I... I—" I felt a lump steadily growing in my throat, threatening to block out my passageway, like trying to speak through a blocked straw. "I just wanted a chance to prove—"

"Girls like you are all the same, and as you spend your time here in your ill-gotten seat, think about how many of your professors may know how different you are from the other students in their classes." The older woman practically spat, the clicking of her heels growing quieter and quieter as she clacked out of of the room, leaving me alone with my thoughts in the lecture hall.

There was something about Dr. Cross' judgmental gaze that reminded me vaguely of my father; how he used to tell me I was too stupid to ever amount to anything on my own, and the best that I could hope for was finding a man like him to take care of me till I die.

Is that what I did? It was with crumbling acceptance that I realized—yes, that is what I did. I couldn't get what I wanted, so I used my body to get it instead. Meeting Damien had turned me into the one thing I never wanted to be.

Yeah, I got into Stanford, but at what cost?

Could I even be proud of it?

Damien

There was a new voicemail from Morgan when I woke up that morning. For months, she had been leaving me sporadic messages, trying to have some sort of heart-to-heart. In truth, there was nothing left to talk about. She'd said everything there was to say the last time we'd spoken.

She was right about me. I saw a girl in a precarious situation, and I took advantage of her. I knew what I was doing was fucked up, but I rationalized it by constantly reminding myself that she was for sale anyway. All the while, she was cracking under the role I'd relegated her to. I took her to a dark place and didn't care because I refused to see her as a person. It was a fucked up thing for me to do and there was no coming back from that.

No matter how longing her voicemails sounded.

Morgan herself had said she had Stockholm Syndrome. These pining messages on my phone, that I, for some reason, refused to delete even after hearing them, were just manifestations of the unnatural attachment she'd developed as a result of my twisted captivity.

I pressed the speaker button on my phone, and her voice filled my apartment.

"Tomorrow's my 1L Orientation." She sighed. "I can't believe it's really happening, and it dawned on me today that I never said thank you. You're probably not going to return this call either, but you haven't changed your number yet, so I'm assuming you're listening to these messages. Remember when you said that if I was vulnerable, you would never hurt me? This is me being vulnerable—I miss you. And it hurts me that you won't talk to me."

She should've hated me. Shit—I hated me for her.

But with every message sent, she ate away at my resolve, and this was the one that tipped the scale. There was something about her voice that moved me. It made me admit to myself that, even after all this time...

I missed her.

Maybe just a little.

After mulling over it in my office for hours, I finally dialed the number. It rang three times before she picked up.

"Hello?" There was a hint of disbelief to her tone. The sound of her voice feeding back live through the phone speaker—it hit me like an oncoming train. But a general calmness fell over me, like all was right in the world; I had no idea a voice could do that to a person.

I asked the first thing that came to mind. "How was your first day?"

There was a pause on Morgan's end before she finally spoke. It sounded like she'd been crying. "Awful. My father... he was right about me. He always used to say my best bet was finding a man to take care of me, because I'd never be able to amount to anything on my own. I wanted to prove him wrong so bad—that... that... that I proved him right."

Good Father

Damien

"Morgan, I'm going to tell you something and it's going to sound harsh, but it's just the honest truth," I finally spoke, trying not to let the sounds of her sobbing breaths get to me. "I wouldn't have lifted a finger to get you into that school if I didn't already know you were qualified—"

"You got me in because I slept with you," she argued.

"I got you in because you were never supposed to have been rejected in the first place," I corrected firmly. "I slept with you because I'm an asshole, and I saw an opportunity to get something I wanted without much effort. You were desperate, and I took advantage of that—knowing your rejection wasn't even fair to begin with. I'd apologize again, but I have a sneaking suspicion that you would forgive me, so I won't.

"Here's the thing, Morgan—this version of you—the one that's been blowing up my phone for the past few months, I don't know her. The girl I met was this... entitled, spoiled brat who didn't know how to take no for an answer and had a smart-mouthed remark for everything I said. Despite what I said about wanting you submissive, there was nothing wrong with that girl I met first. I don't know what you need to do to get her back, but you should work on it. Next time I talk to you, I want to talk to her, or not at all. And as for Stanford, I know for a fact that there's a post-enrollment scholarship named after me this year. If you want to prove that you belong there—get it."

I wanted to tell her that she was smart and capable and perfectly deserving of the space she occupied in that school, but I also longed for the version of her that didn't need me to say these things to already know them about herself.

"I did *something* to you—something that *changed* you—and I hate it," I confessed. "And I can't sit here on the phone and listen to how much I have... *ruined* you, and act like that shit doesn't bother me. You *miss* me? You miss someone who practically reenacted your rape? You miss someone who damn near broke your wrist? Fuck that, Morgan. There's a version of you twisting around in her grave at the woman who you've become. *That's* who I miss."

If I was being honest with myself, Morgan was broken long before she met me. I was merely the gust of wind that sent her delicate house of cards tumbling. If there was anything in the world that

I owed her, it was a little bit of help building that house back up.

And this time, we were going to build with something a little more substantial than cards.

———

There were so many portrayals of me in the media as this cold-blooded sociopath.

Over time, I've grown tired of trying hard to disprove these misconceptions of me. The people I knew, they were acquainted with the milder side of me. The people I didn't, they could get exactly the person they expected me to be.

Years and years of dealing with my infamous persona taught me it could come in handy when necessary. For Morgan, I could be a monster.

I already have been.

"Mr. Jean-Baptiste will see you now." The thin secretary in the all-black dress suit vaguely reminded me of Morgan. It made me wonder if he'd developed a type before or after he'd raped her. I tried not to think about it, as I needed to enter this meeting with a clear head.

It had taken me three months to get into the room with this man; three months since I'd last spoken to Morgan. She was presumably hitting the law books, trying to win my namesake scholarship. Quietly, I was making my own moves behind the scenes. Today, was a culmination of all my efforts.

"Ahh, Mr. Fine." A stout man stood from behind a spotless desk when I entered, extending a hand out for me to shake. I took it with a straight face, feeling his firm grip squeeze my fingers and I couldn't help but think about how much bigger he was compared to Morgan, couldn't help but think about how she was likely even smaller when she was seventeen. "So good of you to come."

I took a seat on the empty chair opposite his desk. The easiest way to get a meeting with a politician is to hint at a possible campaign contribution. He eyed the briefcase I'd come in with, a glimmer of excitement in his eyes at the possibility of receiving a political bribe. He didn't seem to care about my reputation. Senators love nothing else if not their billionaires.

"As you know, I am running for re-election next year and—"

"No." I stopped him. "I'm not here to talk about that."

He was quiet as I opened up that briefcase, eyes still glimmering with that hopeful sheen of riches to come. Inside the briefcase was a single gun, encased within a plastic Ziploc bag. I watched his face fall, and that hopeful glimmer morphed quickly into fear.

"*Don't*—do anything rash," I advised calmly. "You're going to want to hear this. First, take the gun out of the briefcase." He didn't move. "Would you rather I have the gun, or you?" I questioned.

Of course, like the coward I knew he would be, he chose the latter, snatching up the gun from the briefcase and stuffing it in his desk.

"What's this all about?" He was already slightly outraged.

"You have a daughter who's a junior at Spelman College, correct?" I asked, already knowing he did. "She wants a career in finance, as you may know. And, for the past three months, she's been an intern at the Atlanta offices of Fine Investments. Astrid, is it?"

The senator's eyes narrowed with concern, and I motioned toward his seat before taking my own.

"You had an intern yourself in your first year as mayor, didn't you? Before you became a senator. Do you remember her name?"

I let the silence that followed hang in the air. The man shook his head unconvincingly.

"Oh, don't give me that—she was your best friend's daughter. Of course you remember her name." I shook my head, my eyes zeroing in on his before I asked, "Do you remember what you did to her?"

"I—I'm not sure I know what—"

"'*Good heavens, were you a virgin?*'" I quoted. "What a fucked up thing to say to the *child* you've just raped."

He opened his mouth to speak.

"Don't deny it." I lifted a hand to stop him. "That would just piss me off. She says that's what happened—and I *believe* her."

The senator pressed his lips together, deciding not to test my patience. One, because he could see I wouldn't tolerate it, and two, because we *both* knew Morgan wasn't lying.

"So, here's what's going to happen," I started. "For the past three months, your daughter has been a willing participant in several financial crimes, using information that's been fed to her at the Atlanta office. I don't blame her. There she is, with stock market cheat codes and a get rich quick scheme that's practically infallible. Even the best of us might succumb to the temptation.

"She thinks that several of the office workers are doing it, but no... it's just her. It must calm her guilty conscience to think she's not the only one gaming the system, who knows? What you *should* know is that she's been leaving a paper trail and all it would take is for one person to report her and bam—we could be looking at a white collar felony charge. No future for Miss Astrid Jean-Baptiste. Maybe even some extensive jail time.

"You love your daughter, don't you?" He didn't answer, but he sat frozen in his seat. "Lucky her. Some of us aren't born so lucky. Some of us don't get fathers who give a shit about us. As I'm sure you know. Morgan's father didn't love his daughter as much as you clearly love yours." I leaned forward in my chair. "But enough about that. Let's get to the point, Senator."

"Because I am a generous person, I'm going to give you thirty days. As a show of good faith. In that time, I need for you to call that old friend of yours and tell him exactly what you did to his daughter. Be as descriptive as possible. He needs to hear it. And shortly after you speak to him, I need you to take that gun in your desk, put it in your mouth, and blow your brains out—"

The man across from me laughed incredulously, but there was fear in the way his eyes danced across the room. He shifted nervously in his seat. "You're ridiculous."

"No," I shook my head. "I'm dead serious."

"You want me to blow my brains out because you say so?" More shifting. "Over the word of some little girl who says I—"

"She's not little anymore, but it's sick that that's how you remember her," I cut in and he was silent again. "You're going to do it because if you don't, I will use every available resource I have to make sure the story gets told anyway. And shortly after your baby girl Astrid finds out that her daddy is a pedophile rapist, she's going to get booked for insider trading. She's going to tell people she got the intel at the office, but like I said... nobody at the office, but her, is making trades off that intel, so the public is going to think she got insider info from her rapist senator father. They're gonna throw the book at her. Hard.

"But all that can be avoided if you just do as I say. Either way—you're fucked. It's just that, in my preferred method, the only person who goes down is you and your daughter gets to keep all that illegal money she's made." I shrugged. "You wouldn't want to hurt your own child now, would you, senator? I certainly wouldn't want to harm one of *my* interns. Why don't you make it easier for the both of us?"

The man behind the desk had tears pooling over at the rims of his eyes. I couldn't tell if it was terror, remorse, anger, or all three.

"You have thirty days. That's more than enough time to get your affairs in order. If you'd like—you can call your daughter, and maybe ask her why it's been a minute since she's called you for money... That'll show you that I'm not bluffing." I rose from the seat, leaving the empty briefcase on his desk.

In parting, all I said was, "Why don't you show me how good of a father you can be. Like I said—some of us aren't so lucky."

I'm Speaking

Morgan

For nearly four months, I ate, slept, and breathed my studies.

The top ten students were to be awarded a full-ride scholarship, and if there was anything that was going to prove to Dr. Cross—and to myself—that I belonged here, being one of those students would do the trick. I strived for perfection on every assignment. I didn't even make friends, I made study partners.

Damien was pushed to the far ends of my mind, and while I would think of him from time to time, my thoughts would often wander to the memory of him telling me that he missed me, but not me—he missed the version of me that didn't even like him. He wanted to talk to a version of me that had no desire to belong to any man. It was never going to work.

I cut my losses and decided to focus on what was important—school.

It was the last week of the first semester. A busy fifteen weeks it had been, with no time for anything but hitting the books and sleep, and sometimes not even sleep.

Final exams had come and passed and today the list of Fine Scholars was going to be posted just outside of Dr. Cross' office in the financial aid building. Dozens of students were crowded around a single sheet of paper when I arrived at the dimly lit hallway, where the bulletin board was hung.

One by one, students walked up to the single white sheet pinned to the board. Most of them turned back disappointed, the light leaving their eyes as they accepted their defeat. Not wanting an audience when I checked, I leaned against the back wall, waiting for the eager students to clear out one by one before stepping to the bulletin board myself.

A numbered list of ten students' names, and none of them were mine.

At least three of the names on the list, I knew I was doing better than academically. They were in my study groups—I'd been the one to tutor some of them on occasion. It didn't make sense for their names to be on the list and not mine. I read the list ten more times, hoping I'd somehow overlooked my name the first nine times.

Nothing. All that effort I put in. For nothing.

The shock of it all might've left me temporarily insane because I found myself barging into Dr.

Cross' adjacent office, outraged etched deep into my features. Something unjust was taking place here.

Dr. Cross was seated behind her desk with a stack of papers at her chest. In her hand, she held a pen between her teeth as she slowly looked up to find me standing in her office, anger radiating off of me like steam.

"Morgan," she greeted flatly. I'd seen her around campus all throughout the semester, but today was the first time since orientation that she was addressing me directly. "Can I help you?"

I cut straight to the chase. "Why am I not a Fine Scholar?"

Dr. Cross stifled a short chuckle. "You really have to ask?"

"I have the grades, I have the test scores, I have the—"

"Morgan." She stopped me with a hand. "As an aspiring lawyer, surely you understand the conflict of interest it would be to award scholarship money to a student affiliated with the donor."

"What?"

"As with any cash prize—friends and family are ineligible." Dr. Cross widened her eyes. "What did you think this was?"

"He's *not* my friend," I argued. "I barely know him." Especially now.

"Need I remind you, Damien Fine phoned a favor in with the dean for you to get you into this school," Martina reminded. "You're plenty acquainted enough. You're ineligible." She waved a dismissive hand. "And before you get any bright money-making ideas, please be aware that you may be expelled from this institution if your conduct outside of it brings any untoward attention to us."

"I shut down my website a long time ago."

"Good. Don't start it back up." It was easy to tell that she was getting ready to dismiss me. "Shut the door on your way out."

I snapped. "But I earned it! I earned that scholarship fair and square because I studied hard, and I belong here. I earned it."

"Is that what this is about for you?" Dr. Cross wondered. "Then fare thee well, Morgan. You are a smart little cookie and if you'd like, I'll print out a certificate *just* for you. I know exactly what it should say. Morgan Caplan—smartest prostitute at Stanford Law."

I spoke through gritted teeth. "I. Am. Not. A. Prostitute."

"Hm," Martina mused. "Anymore."

"No," I shouted, not caring if my voice carried down the halls outside. "I was never selling myself, I was selling an *idea*. You can sit in that seat and look down on me all you want, but I'm not going to apologize for doing what I had to do to survive out here. So what, if Damien called a favor in for me? You're the last person in the world who should be judging me for it." I reached for the door before asking, "Didn't he do the same for you?"

"Did you hear about Mr. Jean-Baptiste?" Lauren's voice filled my tiny studio as I stewed over the happenings of the day. I had only picked up her call because I was badly in need of someone to vent to. The last thing I needed was my sister saying *that name* to me when I was already in a foul mood. "He shot himself a few hours ago. It's all over the news."

"*What?*" It felt like something unlatched in my chest—as if, for the longest time, something had been squeezing my heart and from the moment I heard the news, it let go. "Is he dead?"

"Afraid so," Lauren confirmed. I never told my sister what he did to me when we were younger; I didn't plan on it. "He didn't leave a note or anything. Just... gone."

"That's..." I couldn't find a word that I could use out loud. *Great news. Amazing. The best thing I've heard all day.* "That's... Poor Astrid. I remember she was such a daddy's girl."

"Are *you* gonna be alright?" Lauren asked. In my hand, my phone lit up with a second call. An unsaved number, but I recognized the number well enough to not need caller ID to know who it was. My breath caught in my throat and I broke out into a nervous sweat. Lauren continued to talk, "I know you worked with him that one time and—"

"Lauren, I have to call you back. I'm getting another phone call—" I swallowed audibly. "—from dad."

I didn't give my sister enough time to react before I pressed the green button on the screen. I barely spoke two syllables before my father cut me off. "Hello—"

"So, how'd you do it?" It was the first time I'd heard my father's voice in years and his tone was venomously accusatory to start. I was confused. "You threaten the man with some hashtag Me Too bullshit?"

"Is this about—"

He wouldn't let me get a word in.

"An hour before the news broke, I got a call from Herschel. He was talking to me like he was being held at gunpoint, telling me this *absolutely disgusting* story about what you did together—"

"Together?" I cut him off then. "Did he tell you we did it together, or did he tell you he did it to me? Because I assure you there is a *fucking* difference!"

"*What* did you do Morgan?" He was ignoring the point. "What did you do to Herschel?"

"I'm in California!" I shouted over him. "I haven't been in Florida in over six months. I haven't even spoken to that man since I was seventeen! I'm in California, going to a school I didn't even want to be at because I've been chasing this phone call for years. Except in my dreams, you were congratulating me for getting into this fucking school, not crying and yelling at me because your disgusting bestie blew his fucking brains out!"

"Morgan—"

"No, shut the fuck up, Dad. I'm speaking!" I screamed. For the first time in my life, I was speaking to my father the way I used to talk to every other man, wishing I could speak to him this way. "Your friend calls you and confirms that yes, he in fact did rape your seventeen-year-old daughter and instead of calling me and begging me for forgiveness, you pull this shit.

"But then again, you don't have to believe me now because you believed me then! You just didn't care! Because to you didn't think I was worth the fuss. Because for whatever reason, you have hated me for as long as I can remember, but there's nothing wrong with me, Dad! There was never anything wrong with me! There's something wrong with you!

"You have issues you need to work out, and you should've never been *anybody's* father! You cared about your friendship with that man more than your own daughter! Well, if you love your fucking friend so much, how about you do us all a favor and join him in hell!"

I hung up, desperate to have the last word.

My chest was still heaving from panting breaths as I dialed in the next number onto my phone screen. It rang three times before he answered.

"Hello," Damien's voice spoke from the other side. At the sound of his voice, my racing heart only picked up. I said the first thing that came to mind.

"Please tell me you didn't do anything that could get you into trouble."

"Why are you breathing so fast?" Damien asked curiously, like he hadn't heard my initial question. "Slow down, Mistress Morgan. It sounds like you're having a panic attack."

"Where... are... you?" I asked, trying to slow my hyperventilating chest.

Damien waited for my breaths to slow before he spoke again, tone calm, if not slightly amused. "I'm in California."

Conquered

Morgan

"In California? How long have you been here?"

"I flew in just last night," his voice fed back through the speakers. Good—so he was nowhere near Florida when that man... *Good*. Relief was washing over me like a wave, although I had no idea what I was expecting. It was presumptuous of me to even think Damien might kill a man for me. He didn't seem to have the slightest idea what all my commotion was about either. "Law school teaching you to start every conversation with established alibis, or are you just an over achiever?"

"Sorry, I thought..." I trailed off unsure of how to tell him exactly what I had thought. "He's dead. He shot himself this afternoon, but my dad—my dad said he sounded like he didn't... he didn't want to and I... I... I thought maybe..."

"Hey." His deep voice was soothing, seemingly softened just for my benefit. "Slow down, Morgan. Breathe. What are you asking me?"

"I thought maybe you—" I didn't dare finish that sentence. "I don't know—I don't know—it's actually kind of stupid."

"It can't hurt to ask."

But it just might.

I thought about apologizing for taking up his time, thought about hinting that now was a good moment for him to exit from the awkwardly random call, but I hesitated, hearing his steady breaths against my ear. My eyes closed to the sound, almost feeling the warmth of his exhales against my neck.

Damien waited. I felt as though I should dismiss myself to go another several months without talking to him, but instead, I curiously asked, "Why are you in California?"

He didn't seem like he was in a hurry to get off the phone either. "I'm in town for an event for *your* school, actually."

To his revelation, I made a sound of understanding, knowing that this event must have had something to do with the Fine Scholar program. Long before today, there had been talk that those ten brilliant students were going to be the guests of honor at some fancy banquet where they would rub shoulders with San Francisco's top brass in the legal field. Evidently, it seemed those students would also get to dine with Damien Fine himself.

Lucky them.

"I looked for your name on the guestlist. Imagine my surprise when I didn't find it."

Something in my chest warmed at the realization that he had fully expected me to get that scholarship. He hadn't said so when he suggested that I aim for it, but clearly he didn't doubt my ability to do it. *Damien thinks I'm smart enough*, I realized.

But just like that, everything else that transpired that day came rushing back—the list outside of Dr. Cross' office and the argument that ensued after. I paced around my small studio, gnawing on my lower lip in thought, wondering if it would be appropriate to tell him. I wanted so badly to have someone to vent to about it, and there he was, a ready ear.

I gave it to him straight. "I don't qualify for the scholarship."

"Why not?" There was an edge to Damien's tone, as though he already suspected something unfair was taking place and he was preemptively outraged on my behalf.

"Because I know you, and according to Dr. Cross, that's a conflict of interest—no friends and family, she says."

He spoke candidly. "We're not even friends."

A short laugh escaped me. "I said the *same* thing."

"And that's the only reason you didn't get it?" he questioned.

"Yeah, but... you phoned in a favor to get my rejection appealed," I reminded. "It's not farfetched that they'd think there's some sort of... connection. I think the powers that be at that school have decided you've done enough to help me get ahead—"

"Don't say it like that when you've earned it." He stopped me. "I'm sure you've realized that most of your classmates have... *something* that gives them an advantage over others. Maybe some of them were in the right place at the right time. Maybe some of them knew the right people. Maybe some of them were born with silver spoons in their mouths. Everybody has *something*, Morgan." Damien continued, "You—you just happen to be quite smart and very driven. Except, you keep getting things taken away from you because other people are making the rules up as they see fit."

"You keep talking like that and I just might start to feel sorry for myself." I forced another smile as if he could see the brave face I was trying to put on. "Look—it's whatever at this point. I have enough money saved up to pay for school, and—"

"Why should you have to dry up your savings when you qualify for that scholarship?" he questioned.

"I mean, technically I don't have to do anything if it bothers you so much. You are the Fine in Fine Scholar," I reminded, halfway rolling my eyes. "If you're really so choked up about it—feel free to pay my tuition yourself, Mr. Billionaire."

"Are you asking me to?" He almost sounded so ready to oblige, as if he'd give me whatever my heart desired so long as I asked up front. Asking required vulnerability, and if that's what he wanted from me, then we were still playing those juvenile power games.

"I would never dream of asking you for anything again, Mr. Fine," I replied coolly. "I don't imagine you go around paying people's tuitions for nothing in return, and I don't think it would be wise to get into another mutually beneficial arrangement with you."

"And if all I want in return is an hour of your time?"

"I would say I don't charge by the hour anymore." I let the words hang in the silence that followed, giving him back the Morgan he claimed he missed for only a minute before I added, "You don't have to pay my tuition to take me out on a date, you know."

Asking required vulnerability, so maybe I wasn't all that tired of playing the power games. Maybe I was tired of being the vulnerable one. Today, I'd already stuck up to my father for the first time in my life. The last thing I wanted to do after an accomplishment such as that was grovel at another man's feet for his attention and approval.

No—I'd much rather have a man grovel at mine.

"You just have to ask me."

The first ever time Damien ever asked me anywhere, he didn't ask me if I was willing, he simply told me how long he would wait for me there. Ten minutes he gave me, that first night. Yesterday, he asked me out on a proper date. He didn't even bother teasingly calling me Mistress Morgan like he usually did. It was serious to him. The question was just a straightforward—*"Morgan, would you have dinner with me tomorrow night?"*

The ball was in my court from the moment he popped the question.

A long time ago, tangled in the sheets of Damien's bed, I saw a man ripe for the taking. There was some part of Damien that had to have liked me, but I was unsure if it was purely physical or if there was some emotional motivation as well. If there were any feelings involved, I knew that if I played my cards right, I might bend him to my own will—a sub that didn't sign up to be a sub. Something to be conquered.

For dinner, he invited me to The Ripley, a fancy hotel in the heart of downtown. I assumed it was the hotel he was staying at while he was here, and that he was simply streamlining the journey from this date to his bed. Of course, I had no intention to sleep with him tonight, so he could've invited me for dinner in his bedroom for all I cared. Nothing was going to happen tonight.

My Uber pulled up to the front of the hotel building in the center of the city, a beige bricked structure that climbed all the way up to the clouds. Outside, lots of people were funneling in and out through the lobby in cocktail attire. Two faces I recognized from Stanford whizzed past and into the hotel without even noticing me, dressed in a lavender slip dress that cascaded past my knees with a deep slit. Damien had told me to wear a cocktail dress, but I had assumed that it was the restaurant's dress code, not because I was actually going to a cocktail party.

It wasn't until I'd seen a third recognizable face that I begun to wonder what was going on. Inside the hotel, my questions were answered when I found myself surrounded by dozens Stanford Law faculty. A few of my own professors caught my eye and waved in the middle of their conversations, and I began to feel hot in the face, wondering what Damien had brought me out to.

In the hotel's lobby, hanging over the entrance of a double doored ballroom, was a banner that read, in Stanford maroon, Congratulations to our Fine Scholars. Now my skin felt prickly, wondering if Damien had decided to play some sort of prank on me, but just as I was reeling, I caught the gaze of a familiar faced Dr. Martina Cross.

She was dressed fabulously in a long black dress that draped over her shoulders and back like a cape. It made her look like she was effortlessly gliding as she walked the twenty-foot distance between her and I, the expression on her face absolutely deadly.

"What are *you* doing here?" She spat the word *you*. If Damien was playing a prank on me, this was just cruel.

I started to answer. "I was—"

Dr. Cross cut me off. "I can't believe you thought you could just waltz in here and—"

"Martina." I heard him before I saw him. Just as quickly, I felt a hand rested at the small of my back. It was warm and familiar, so I didn't have to turn over my shoulder to know *he* was who I'd find. "She didn't just waltz in here—she was invited." When I turned to look at him, I was thankful for the hand steadying me at my back, because I felt my knees wobble only just a little. I was reminded of our first date at the FEEL Center, how his hand rested comfortably on my back then, too. This time, however, it felt more personal, as if he wasn't just touching his date—he was touching *me*.

I was suddenly unsure if I could conquer Damien Fine into submission. This was a man who made me weak at the knees.

Clearly, I was already the conquered one.

Damien spoke to Dr. Cross with absolute finality, something about his tone wordlessly warning her to leave me alone—not just now, but in general—as if he could already tell she'd been harassing me for a while. This wasn't a prank on me and his hand at my back slid over to my waist, his hold on me protective. I felt like I was his, and it made me feel safe.

"Morgan isn't here as one of your students, Martina—she's my date this evening. Treat her like you would treat any one of my dates," he said, which felt like a more polite way of saying '*watch the way you talk to her*'. I felt myself smiling, not minding the possessive hold of his hand at my waist.

"Oh..." Martina's hardened expression immediately softened for me. Damien was a friend of hers she clearly did not wish to upset. "My apologies, Morgan, I hadn't realized you were coming tonight."

I hadn't realized I was coming tonight either...

She opened her mouth to say something to her friend, but she took one look at his face and pressed her lips together, deciding saying nothing might be better. She excused herself instead. The moment Martina walked away, I looked up to meet Damien's eyes and he was already looking at me. He asked knowingly, "Really? *That's* who intimidates you?"

"She's intimidating when she's not kissing your ass, I promise." I found myself returning his dazzling smile. "Was inviting me here your idea of a joke? Are you amused?"

"It was my idea of justice, really," he told me, speaking to me as if I were the only guest in the room, as if he couldn't see the dozens of curious eyes on him, eager for an opportunity to get him alone, to pick his mind. I could feel the eyes of both faculty and classmates on me alike. I wondered what they were thinking. "You should be here."

"So that's the only reason you asked me out?" I asked, feeling him guide me away from the thick of the crowd. "To help me network?"

"You sound very ungrateful," he commented, but his faint smile was amused, a twinkle in his eye I felt like was saved specifically for me. Damien's hand at my waist pulled me in further, facing me so close that our noses nearly touched. It was only now that I was realizing that he'd pulled me into a practically empty corridor, leading out of the main ballroom. Against my mouth, he whispered, "And no—that's not the only reason."

"And so?" I asked slowly, wanting to hear the other reasons, so close to him I felt like I could taste the heat on his skin.

Damien didn't answer my question, instead choosing to lean in to close the space between our mouths, softly landing on me tenderly at first. He was soft against me, skin warm to the touch like receiving the best of hugs. And then his lips were ravenous, devouring me with hungry desire, his hand at my waist circling around to my back, holding me to him.

Damien pulled at my lips, opening me up to slide his tongue into my mouth and he tasted like spearmint, choreographing this passionate dance between our mouths, and I kissed him back—equally consumed in passion, equally hungry for him. His movements were slow, taking his time with me as though we would have all the time in the universe to hold each other.

His hands at my back slid down to my backside, grabbing handfuls of my behind through my dress, and I wanted nothing more than for him to lift me up against the wall and take me right then and there, but there was a party going on. His name was on the programs and people were expecting him any moment without my wine red color on his lips. It took an inhuman amount of will power, but I broke the kiss—our *first* ever kiss.

I'd been bedded by this man more times than I could keep track of, but this was the first time he was kissing me. My mind was racing with questions about what this could all mean, but I didn't ask them. Perhaps I feared what the answers might be. There was a sort of bliss in not knowing.

I brought my thumb up to his lips, wiping off the lipstick as he searched for something in my eyes. Maybe he, too, was also looking for answers to questions he was too afraid to ask out loud. His hands were back at my waist when he ducked his head down, bringing his lips close to my ear, and just as I thought he'd press a kiss to my neck, he simply whispered, "I asked you to come, because I missed you."

I hadn't realized how tense I was until those words had my entire body relaxing—relief was what it was. Somehow it was the answer to all the questions swimming around in my head, the reassurance that I needed. However, his words also crafted a new curiosity within me and I didn't have the slightest idea how to answer the new question he left me with.

Who gets to be the dominant when both of us have been conquered by the other?

YOURS

MORGAN

Damien pulled my chair out for a seat beside him at the banquet table. The placard on my plate read: **Martina Cross** in gold foil script. When he saw me reading it with worry between my brows, he confidently assured, "She'll find a new seat."

Damien was supposed to have been talking to scholars all night.

They were young, ambitious law students, eager to make their mark on the world, eager to rub shoulders with as many powerful people as they could find. The most powerful person in the room just didn't seem to care about anyone else in attendance.

Martina, now sitting at the end of the table tried to introduce the students to Damien one-by-one, and he offered each a nod, congratulating them for their efforts. He seemed disinterested and bored all night unless talking to me.

If I were a Fine Scholar, I would've hated me right about now. I received their dirty looks with a smile.

At some point in the middle of the evening, one of my classmates by the name of Rei asked while dessert was being served, "How do you two know each other? I always thought Morgan seemed so to herself."

I felt my eyes narrow. Maybe I just don't like y'all.

"We met on the internet," Damien answered vaguely, a hint of a smile threatening to break out onto his features. He thought that was funny. "It's how everyone is meeting these days."

Underneath the table, I could feel his hand slide against my outer thigh. It made my back go rigid at first, but I tried not to make it obvious to the other guests at the table. Little by little, his hand moved into the long slit of my dress, inching toward the inner skin of my thighs.

"Oh wow—the internet. Talk about luck," Rei congratulated me for my great catch, as Damien's hand slid further up my dress. I tried to keep my breathing steady.

"Yes," Damien agreed, his eyes never once leaving my face. "I *am* very lucky."

When his fingers reached the fabric of my panties, I drew in a long breath, looking down at my plate so that my face would not give me away. Damien was multitasking—feeling me up under the table and responding to students and faculty who wished to get on his good side. There was opportunity in befriending a man like Damien. Of all people, I would know.

I could feel myself pooling in my underwear, so much of me had been craving his touch these last few months, and I was nearly coming undone at the mere glide of his thumb against the wet spot in my panties.

I couldn't focus on anything that was being discussed at the table. The only thing I could do was bite my lower lip hard so that I would not moan in the middle of this dinner. Damien seemed determined to make me do it anyway.

"...and it's a pity what happened to that senator down in Florida," Martina's voice cut through the haze cloud in my head. Damien's thumb against me paused.

"We all have to die someday," he replied, something unreadable about his tone. I wondered if he even remembered that the senator was the same man who violated me all those years ago. There were grumbles at the table at Damien's crass choice of words for a man dead by suicide. "Look at the bright side—at least he got to choose right until the very end."

Oh, he definitely remembered.

In spite of myself, I chuckled, and as if I had moaned in the middle of dinner, all eyes were on me then. "What? That was funny."

"A man has died and you're cracking jokes." Martina shook her head disapprovingly as Damien shrugged, his hand slipping away from between my thighs. In a move nobody else at the table would fully understand, he brought his thumb to his lips, slowly running his tongue along half of it. It maybe lasted a second and a half for everyone else watching, but for me it was like it was happening in slow motion.

I needed to go to the bathroom, to cool myself down somehow, but part of me wanted him to follow. Dinner was practically over, and I just wanted to get him away from the swarming social climbers and have him all to myself. Damien's eyes followed me as I quietly excused myself from the table, and I could somehow feel them on me all the way to the bathroom.

The water running from the faucet in the ladies room was cold. There were nobody else in the stalls or at the sink to make small talk as I splashed my face with cool water half a dozen times, letting my cold hands run down my neck and shoulders. Never in my life had I been so attracted to someone to the point that my skin felt like it was on fire.

I stood in that bathroom for several minutes, timing in my head how now should be the time they would start rising from their seats. Now should be the time Damien would be making his way to the bathroom. Now should be the time that door was opening.

None of that happened.

I grabbed my purse off the bathroom counter, heading for the exit, coming face-to-chest with a man in a suit as soon as I opened the door. *Wow, I did not time that correctly*, I thought, looking up to find Damien's blazing dark eyes. Neither of us said anything as I stepped several paces back while he stepped in, locking the door behind him.

"Is it over?" I asked. "The party."

"Were you waiting it out?" he asked, almost smiling, hand reaching for my waist before pulling me up onto the bathroom counter. "I had no idea you were so anti-social."

"It's this school," I muttered as he drew the hem of my skirt up. I leaned back against the bathroom mirror behind me. "Dr. Cross makes it seem like everyone on faculty is secretly judging me for sleeping my way to the top. Makes me uncomfortable—" his hands drew up my thighs "—like I can never fully relax in this place. It really sucks.

Damien's thumb slipped into the waistband of my panties, pulling them down over my knees and then past my heels. He took the black lace garment and stuffed it in his pocket, like he planned on keeping it forever. In an instant, his lips were back on mine, taking me by surprise at first because this was new for us, all this kissing.

I tried to tell him between kisses. "I was thinking..." He slipped a finger into me as he took my lips back into his. "...about finishing off this year..." he kissed me again, cutting me off, pushing in a second. "...and then just transferring to a school in Miami."

Damien pulled back.

"All that work you did to get in just to throw it away because of Martina?" he asked.

I shook my head, still feeling myself wrapped around his two inserted fingers. "*Not* because of her. I never wanted to come to Stanford for the right reasons anyway. And I miss home."

Damien nodded, respecting my decision by not trying to talk me out of it. Besides, I think he was thinking about how convenient it would be for us to be in the same city again.

"Do you need anything from me?" He offered up his help.

My heart fluttered, but I shook my head. "You can't ask me that with your hand up my skirt. How will I ever beat the sleeping my way to the top allegations?"

Damien laughed, closing the space between us again. He tasted like the berry flavor of my lipstick, the dips and pulls of his mouth moving against mine with the same deliberate slowness as his hand between my thighs.

The way he touched me had changed, I noted, moaning into his mouth as his thumb passed over my ready clit, rubbing me rhythmically. All of this was for my benefit, as though I were just here to receive. That's what had changed. When he pulled back from my lips, he encouraged, "Then sleep your way to the top. I'm not complaining about what I get out of it. Make your demands, Mistress Morgan."

I smiled against his lips. "You always sound like you're mocking me when you call me that."

"Would it sound more convincing on my knees?"

I shook my head, whispering, "Don't ever get on your knees for me."

This was how I liked us, in that gray space where neither of us had a role. I didn't want to create a new submissive. Especially not one out of Damien.

"I might have to get on my knees once in a while," he reasoned before descending to the bathroom floor, on his knees to get face-to-face with the nakedness underneath my skirt. His hands pulled at my waist to bring me closer to the table's edge before his head disappeared into the lavender fabric of my dress. The first touch of his tongue to me was like an ocean wave washing over me in the Florida heat.

I basked in that familiar warmth and softness I'd grown accustomed to in the month we spent together. Lightly, I panted as his hands found mine, his fingers intertwining into my own, holding my hand as he licked me expertly. I did all I could not to moan loudly in this public bathroom.

"I missed you," I told him as he lapped away at my sex, sending climactic shocks rippling through me that had me squirming on the table. His momentum increased with each moan that quietly left my mouth, eager to sent me over the edge in ecstasy. I came once, gasping as I proclaimed, "Mr. Fine, I missed you so damn much."

He didn't say anything, and I suspected I'd upset him by admitting it. The Morgan he wanted was distant and cold—she wasn't supposed to miss him. He resented that. Still, Damien didn't pull back from my body and his hand remained in mine.

Just before questions could form in my worrisome mind, he guided my hand to the back of his head, and under my skirt he said, "You *can* call me Damien."

"I can?"

I felt him nod against my inner thigh before he pressed a kiss on the sensitive skin there. "You can call me whatever you want."

I didn't push him back to me like he might've expected me to. Instead, my hand slipped from the back of his head and I urged him to come up and look at me. "Damien."

"Hm?"

"What are we?"

Damien emerged from underneath my dress then, the lower half of his face shining with my essence. He brought a hand up to his close-cut facial hair, wiping some of me off before he answered, "I have no idea, Morgan." Something disappointed twisted in my stomach before he added, "I only know what I am."

"And what are you?" I wondered.

His answer was simple.

"Yours."

MINE

MORGAN

"Are you really?" I asked, something apprehensive about my voice. I didn't want my heart to burst with joy, just to realize I'd misunderstood him. *Is he really mine?*

Damien's head tilted to the side, hearing the disbelief in my question. He stepped closer to me; our heights leveled out as I sat on the bathroom counter. His hand cupped my face, thumb gently caressing my cheek when he promised, "I've been yours since that morning, when you walked into my office wrapped in a bedsheet and all I could think about was—I could get used to this."

Against his lips I asked, "Where are you staying tonight?"

"Upstairs." His eyes flickered upward. "On the thirty-fifth floor."

And that was how we found ourselves making out in a private Ripley Hotel elevator. I never used to appreciate how convenient Damien's penchant for private lifts was until that moment. Our uninterrupted ascension to his hotel suite was peak convenience, not having to worry about someone walking in on us as Damien's hand roamed the length of my body.

My hand slipped between the both of us, over the front of his black dress pants, cupping the bulge of him and he inhaled sharply against my mouth.

"Fuck," he murmured against my lips before grabbing my wrist to hold me closer against him, his hips jerking needily and I realized without his assurance, as he rode my palm, that he really *was* mine. He craved my touch just as much if not more than I wanted his.

Again, his lips covered mine, moaning low into my throat, his thrusts against me hungry and desirous as his free hand rose to cup my breast. I whimpered into his mouth, feeling my nipple pebble underneath his fingers, body throbbing and aching as we rode the high of our mutual pleasure.

I thought we wouldn't make it to his room, that I might let him fuck me right here on this elevator. But sure enough, the ding of the elevator sounded off, announcing our arrival to the thirty-fifth floor. Damien pulled gently at my waist, guiding me to his suite.

"This place is bigger than my apartment."

Damien made a face at my admission, hands still possessively holding my waist. "How *small* is your apartment?"

I shook my head, bluntly emphasizing, "Small."

"Stay here then. When I'm gone, you can keep my suite. I'll keep my card on file."

"No... No, I don't want to get comfortable here," I replied, touched by his sweet offer. "If you want to gift me a place to stay, look for something for me in Miami; something close to UM's law school."

"You're really serious about giving up Stanford," he marveled. "After everything you did to get in."

"It led me to you, didn't it?" I reminded, letting him lead me into his bedroom. "I don't regret anything. This school is just not for me, so I'm going home. Now please—" I drew in a deep breath. "—*please* touch me.

His eyes on me focused. Damien had a way of looking at me that spoke the word *'beautiful'* with his eyes alone. His hand at my waist slid down to the slit in my dress, his fingers finding the bareness underneath as my panties were still in his pocket. For him, I was drenched at this point, knowing he must've known from the way his long finger slid effortlessly through my soaked folds.

Just a little bit, he rubbed me slow, but nowhere near enough. His teasing touch was driving me mad. I bit my lip, swallowing his name before I could moan it out, but when he found my clit, my legs began to shake, and his name burst out of me like an explosion. I buried my head into his shoulder, aware that my face was twisting and shifting in pleasure. Damien's free hand drew up to my chin and he guided my eyes back to his.

"Look at me when you cum," he demanded, finger still swirling around my throbbing clit. Each wave was hitting me hard, sending my body into involuntary twitch motions, but he didn't let up. "That feel good, baby?"

And just like that, I never wanted to be Mistress Morgan again. I wanted to be *baby*. Forever. "God, you are—"

He swallowed my sentence, his lips on mine hot and perfectly fitted. I closed my eyes, tasting me on his skin, loving every second of his mouth maneuvering around mine, leading me closer to his bed. His steps were guiding me backwards, hand never leaving the heat between my legs as his fingers sped up.

I sucked in deeply, and Damien pulled back to see my face, fingers continuing to speed up as he encouraged, "Yes, baby. Just like that. Cum for me just like that."

The momentum of his hand didn't slow, rubbing on my clit quickly, and even when I wanted to, I didn't shut my eyes, keeping my gaze on him just like he'd asked. My body tensed, my fingers digging into the front of his shirt as every muscle in my body froze. I was suspended in pure ecstasy, so much so that I was silent, completely losing my voice for a moment before I ultimately cried out his name, long and high pitched.

In the throes of one of the most powerful orgasms I'd ever been given in my life, Damien finally pushed into me. He buried each and every girthy inch in, using the distraction of my climax to numb what should've been excruciating after not having a man enter me in months, but it only made my orgasm more powerful. His eyes were in mine, watching every reaction as I felt my pussy begin to quiver around him.

"Yes," I encouraged. "Fill me up. It's all for you—I'm yours, too!"

The words falling out of me were just as involuntary as the way my body twitched in his hands. Damien smiled a little, holding my gaze for those first slow thrusts. This was not just sex. This was love. I was absolutely convinced. Neither of us had ever said the word, but we didn't have to. Love was in the way he held me as he drove in and out of me. Love was in the way I held him to my chest, watching the fire burn in his eyes, thinking about how I wanted to lay here with him forever.

I felt his body tense in my hands, and I understood he was close. I ran a hand up his back, stopping at the back of his head and when all his muscles seized, he buried his face into my neck and moaned my name long and low as every bit of his seed warmed my insides. This was not just sex. This was—

"I love you," he whispered close to my ear.

Damien Fine is mine.

<hr />

Damien

I couldn't stay in California long.

Work was calling and just because I would've rather stayed in bed with Morgan, didn't mean that

I could. Leaving her behind, however, really made me see the bright side in her moving back to Florida. I spent my entire flight back searching for real estate agents in the Miami area. In my mind, I would get Morgan a little house by her school, in a safe neighborhood, where she could make the space her own.

Someplace I could visit often.

Even though I didn't like the idea of her trading a Stanford law degree for a UM law degree, I already knew I was going to do everything in my power to make sure all of her dreams came true. If she wanted to go to UM because being home made her happier, then she could do that. I hoped she knew she didn't have to worry about the future any longer.

Of course, I knew her well enough to know I should never tell her that. She was a brilliant person, and maybe she didn't realize that I knew it. I was going to help her because she deserved it—not because I had feelings for her. Morgan was too independent minded to openly accept all the help I was willing to give her career wise. I'd have to ease her into it.

I was going to take care of her.

When I arrived at my apartment late Sunday afternoon, Sebastien was waiting for me by the door. He would always come when he needed money. For months, he had been going through my assistant.

On my dime, Chloe would give him small sums here and there, but today was Sunday.

Chloe didn't work on Sundays, but she must've told him I was home today.

It had been a really long time since I'd seen him. Sebastien had been avoiding me ever since I punched him in the face over what he said to Morgan. He'd gotten so thin that his cheeks were now sunken in, but it didn't move me the way it might've in the past.

I had a habit of treating my younger brother like a child, but in truth, he was a few months older than Morgan. I certainly didn't see Morgan as a child. She was so damn self-sufficient and willing to do it all on her own. It made my brother's weekly visits to me or my assistant all the more infuriating. Why couldn't he be as self-sufficient? Because he was using me as a crutch, that's why.

While I wanted to take care of Morgan, it wasn't lost on me that she definitely wasn't asking me to.

"If you're here for money—the answer is no."

"But I'm not high, Dame," Sebastien reasoned, as if this were all the reason I needed to allow him to get high. As if he'd done a good job by not doing any drugs before he got here and his reward to himself would be drugs when he left. "You said I—"

"Look," I said, stopping at my door. "This has got to stop. It's not sustainable and I'm hurting you more than I am helping you. I'll pay for rehab. I'll pay for housing. I'll pay for school. But I'm done bankrolling this drug habit."

He scowled. "Where's all this coming from?"

"I don't have to explain myself to you, Sebastien. It is what it is. I'm about to walk into my apartment, and you're not going to follow in after me, understand?"

There was a silent promise to lay hands on him if he tried it. I'm sure he understood.

"So, you're just going to leave me hanging like this?" Sebastien asked, completely ignoring all the other things I'd offered him instead.

Rather than argue, I just nodded. "Sure—I'm just gonna leave you hanging."

I timed it in my head—*in three, two, one...*

"Fuck you, Damien." "Yeah I know, fuck me." We said it at the same time.

As I let myself into my apartment, I made a mental note to change the passcode for my elevator. I refused to get anymore unsolicited visits from Sebastien from here on out.

He had some growing up to do.

OURS

MORGAN

"Where do you want me to put this?" Damien was carefully holding silver framed mirror. I was sitting at the kitchen island, looking over some pre-2L required reading. I thought about it, looking over the way his muscled arms made the sleeves of his gray t-shirt tight at the ends. My smile was slow, admiring the fact that he wanted to do it all himself as opposed to hiring out the help. In a way, it made him feel more like a boyfriend.

"I think I want that mirror in the foyer, next to the entryway table."

I came home to Miami in the first week of June. A year of law school was secured under my belt, and with a school like Stanford setting my foundations, getting accepted into the University of Miami's law school was practically a given. They wanted me just as bad as I wanted to be there, and here, I'd get the fresh start I needed.

In Miami, I returned to the cutest yellow bungalow just outside of the main law campus. Damien had tailored it specifically to what he'd think I'd need. It wasn't too over the top, but it wasn't cheap by any means. Closed within a white iron fence, the little yellow house was mostly empty when I arrived, ready for my personal touch.

It was half an hour away from the city, but Damien got away from the hustle and bustle of downtown every other day to come see me. He'd said the was mine to decorate as I pleased, but even considering my free reign over the new home, it still felt like the house was *ours*.

I liked that. Feeling like this place was ours made accepting the extravagant gift of a house easier. Accepting a gift of this magnitude would've been impossible for me otherwise. It wasn't surprising for me to discover that Damien was the type to spoil, but even I never expected a house in my name. Grand romantic gestures weren't exactly a thing I was used to getting a man to do without cracking his manhood first, so all of this felt new to me. Damien I were equals—it was like being in a relationship for the first time.

The small house was a maze of boxes, either carrying old things from my storage unit or new furniture pieces to be put together one by one whenever Damien could find the time.

I was spending the summer preparing for a new year at a new school, away from the judgmental eyes of the Stanford faculty—namely Martina. It seemed

I'd be more comfortable here, close to the home I'd always known, close to the man who loved me.

Without making much noise, Damien was back in the kitchen, pulling up a seat across from me at the island.

"Are you sleeping over tonight?" I asked without looking up from my book. There was a tug of hope in my stomach that he might.

He sighed. "Not tonight. I have a couple meetings at the office in the morning, but I'll be back in the evening tomorrow."

Although I wanted him to stay, I liked the fact that he was giving me enough space to still live on my own. All things considered, I was also glad he was never gone for long. Looking up from my reading, I offered him a smile. "Two days in a row for me—you must've broken it off with your other hoes."

"My other hoes," he parroted with a chuckle, sarcastically nodding as he stood to close the gap between us. "Yep, that's it. You just got bumped up to my number one. Congratulations."

Damien pressed a kiss to my forehead in parting, telling me he'd see me soon. I was sinking back into my seat, smiling wondrously at myself at how this was really my life when I heard the front door shut behind him. A minute later, I heard his car start in the front yard.

There was a harsh knocking at the front door the following evening. *Weird*, I thought, because Damien was the only person who knew about this place, and because Damien was supposed to have had a key.

He didn't have to knock, and if he did, he certainly wouldn't have been knocking like the police.

I was in the living room, curled up on a corner of the couch, halfway dozing off when the banging at the door woke me all the way up. When I checked the peephole at the front door, the person standing at the other side was Sebastien, Damien's younger brother.

Now, Damien had told me a thing or two about their strained relationship, but it was obviously a sore spot for him to talk about because he wouldn't volunteer the information freely. I didn't know nearly as much as I would have liked to know. It was the worry that maybe something had happened to Damien that made me open the door. How else would he have known where I lived unless Damien had told him?

"Sebastien—what are you doing here?"

"You." He practically spat the word. My grip on the doorknob tightened. "*You* live here?"

He asked as if he hadn't known this already. "You sound surprised."

"Damien has been coming back and forth from this place for weeks," he indirectly admitted to following his older brother for weeks. "I'm surprised you're still in the picture. This your house?"

"You've been following your brother," I concluded, shrinking some of the gap in the door. This didn't go without him noticing, his eyes darting at the hinges before quickly returning to my face. I felt something in my stomach drop, an omen of danger.

"Mind if I come in?" He asked, not waiting for my response before pushing his way through. I could only watch as he shut and locked the door behind him. "Tell me, Morgan, who paid for this place?"

"That's none of your business."

"So, Damien paid for it," he deduced, stepping closer to me. He was much bigger than I was, and his vibe was frighteningly hostile. I took a step back. "That's really interesting because he's spoiling you—meanwhile the brother he owes, he's leaving high and dry."

Damien said he would be here this evening. I just had to keep Sebastien talking and Damien would be here soon, and he would know what to do. *Just keep him talking.*

"Why does he owe you?"

"Oh, don't act like you don't know." He sounded outraged. "He's famous for it after all." To my confused expression, Sebastien shouted, "My mother!"

"You can't possibly blame him for that." *Just keep him talking.* "I mean—he was just a kid. An abuse victim in his own right. Damien didn't—"

"Are you the one that's been putting all these new ideas in his head? You telling him he did nothing wrong so now he doesn't feel like he owes me for what he did?"

"Damien didn't—"

"*How the fuck* would you know?" Sebastien shouted at me. "Were you there that night? Did you see who lit the match?"

"Damien didn't light the match, and you know it." Sebastien squinted. "Were you there?"

I pressed my lips together tightly as Sebastien looked around the room, appraising things, likely adding up costs in his head. This is where his brother's money had been going instead of to him. By the looks of his face, the realization completely pissed him off.

"How much money you got up in here?" he abruptly cut the silence.

"I don't carry large sums of money." I dug in the back pocket of my jeans. "I have thirteen dollars and a debit card. You can take that, but rest assured that my card has a daily limit."

"I need you to call Damien then. Tell him to bring you ten thousand dollars, and—"

"I'm not doing that," I interrupted smoothly. "You're not about to come into my house and use me to rob your brother. You two obviously have some issues that you need to work out, but I refuse to be put in the middle of—"

"Your house? *Your* house? Bitch—I'll burn *your* fuckin' house to the ground." Sebastian lunged into the space separating us, grabbing me by the shoulders and shaking me. "My savings have run dry. I already sold all my shit. I haven't had a hit of anything in damn near three days. You think I'm playing with you? This is *not* a game. I need that money."

"Let me go." I squirmed between his hands, stuck within his tight grip. *Where is Damien?*

"He can buy you a house, but he can't slide me a little something to make my head stop spinning? Nah, fuck that. You got in his head and made him forget why he owes me, didn't you?"

"What?" I shook my head. "I have no idea what you're talking about."

Sebastien started shaking me again. "None of this mess started until he started seeing you. You come in the picture and suddenly he starts changing his mind about things!"

"That has got nothing to do with me!" I argued back, trying to free myself from his tight grasp. For someone so skinny, he was so strong. "Let me go!"

The harder I squirmed, the harder he shook me, willing me to stand still. The sweat slick on his fingers gave me some leeway and I used my hands to push his chest, hoping to loosen his grip. Sebastien pushed me backward in the foyer and I lost my balance. Behind me the entryway table by the mirror broke my fall, slamming a sharp corner into the back of my head.

I fell to the ground, feeling a wound just above the top of my neck leaking. Warily, I pressed a hand to the back of my hair and when I brought it back to inspect it, my entire hand was painted red.

"Oh fuck," I heard Sebastien swear, hovering above my head, while the corners of my vision were beginning to turn black. I felt outside of myself, in far less pain that I should've been feeling for the amount of blood that was covering my hand.

At my feet, I felt hands wrap around my ankles, dragging me out of the foyer toward the back of the house. My vision was going in and out and my limbs felt like gelatin, leaving me powerless to stop Damien's brother as he dragged me away from the front door. *Where is Damien?*

We were in the kitchen, my head still bleeding out in the middle of the room as Sebastien walked closer to the gas stove.

"That's a nasty gash in the back of your head," Sebastien said aloud, and I was unsure if he was talking to me or just around me, but the next thing I heard him say was, "You probably need to get to a hospital soon, but I can't have you running your mouth and telling people I did that. With my record—they'd throw the book at me."

I wanted to plead, to promise I wouldn't tell anyone. My tongue felt one hundred pounds heavy and I didn't have the strength to move it.

"I can't let anyone see what I did." I didn't even have the strength to properly panic. From afar he started to tell to me, "You know, I once read that those on their deathbed are the best people to confess your sins to. You know how the saying goes—two can keep a secret if one of them is dead. Can I tell you a secret, Morgan?"

I didn't answer. I couldn't answer.

"Damien told the police that he thought our dad started a fire to cover up our mother's death. It wasn't until he heard her screaming that he realized our father hadn't killed her. There's so much about that night that he doesn't know. His room was the furthest away from mom and dad's. I was six—but I remember what they were fighting about."

Through the haze in my head, I was beginning to smell smoke. The only things I had to keep from completely blacking out was that smell, and the sound of Sebastien's voice as he laid his confessions at my feet.

"Dad couldn't afford the house," Sebastien continued. "He was supposed to burn it down so that he wouldn't have to pay for it anymore. He pulled me out of my room in the middle of the night. I was sleepy, too, you know. I saw some matches on the kitchen counter—I was six. I liked fire and explosions. I didn't know... I didn't know Damien and Dad had just poured gasoline all throughout the house. So, I lit one match. It was just supposed to be one and then I'd blow it out. Except... Dad turned around, saw the flame, and shouted, 'what the hell are you doing?' I flinched. I dropped it.

"And then the whole kitchen was in flames. Dad dragged me out to the backyard and he shook me. 'You killed your mother! You killed your brother!' I was only six. I didn't know any better. But then, a miracle—Damien was alive. He didn't save my mom, though. And he thought Dad started the fire. Dad... Dad didn't even bother to explain himself. I suppose the truth sounded too much like a lie... He haunts me, you know. Our dad. He shouts at me over and over again—'You killed your mother! You killed your mother!' That's why I need my pills. It makes him go away... And then it's easier to make Damien think he did it.

"But because of you—My brother won't help me anymore. He's too busy taking care of you. Well shit... my problems started with a fire," Sebastien concluded. "Now maybe I can solve them with a fire."

Never Again

Morgan

It was *so* hot.

The air was thick with black fog, choking me with every inhale. I couldn't breathe without erupting into a fit of coughs. Past the smoke, I could barely see a thing. Beads of sweat were forming at my forehead. Blinded by the dark smoke, I could only gauge the danger from how the heat rose in the room. I tried my best to get back on my feet, but my limbs were unsteady. The back of my head was killing me.

Through the crackling sound of fire moving through the kitchen, I could hear Sebastien leave out the front door, the slamming echoing throughout the near empty house. I would've follow after him, I told myself. The fire hadn't spread through the rest of the house just yet, and if I was going to escape, it had to be soon. But I couldn't stand. I tried and I tried, feeling my vision blur and blacken at the corners.

My arms wobbled and I fell to my chest, completely immobile in the heat.

This is how I die, was my final thought before my eyes shut, resigning to my fate.

"MORGAN!"

My eyes snapped open. Relief blanketed my chest. Damien.

In my head, my name sounded like Damien was shouting it underwater. *I'm in the kitchen!* I thought my response, but I didn't have the voice to say it. My throat was raw from the inhaling of smoke. The room was dark, obscured by black smoke that would've made it impossible to see your hand right in front of you.

I heard my name being called again; this time closer. He was coughing. I felt guilty. Here he was, choking on smoke, in the middle of a burning house because he'd run into one for me. *I'm right here. I'm right here. Please find me.*

On my side, I felt a foot bump into me before stopping. In a moment, I felt strong arms wrap around my body. I couldn't see him through the smoke. In the safety of his arms, the adrenaline keeping me alert died down. My eyes closed and my head slumped against his chest.

The last thing I remember hearing was his soothing voice assuring, "I've got you, baby. I've got you."

There was a mechanical beeping drumming at a repetitive rhythm. Underneath me, I could feel a plush bed. The air was clean but breathing still stung, as if the smoke had followed me here. My chest was sore, something only agitated by the rise and fall of my lungs.

My eyes opened up to a blinding white light, blurred at first but then clearing to find a private hospital room. I swiveled my neck around the room, thinking I was alone at first, until I found Damien seated in an armchair to the side of my bed, eyes on me like he was waiting.

"How—" I stopped talking immediately after realizing how much my throat burned.

"Two days," he answered my question without my finishing it. "You have a bad concussion and a bit of smoke inhalation, but they said you should recover soon."

"Sebastien..." I started to tell him. "He started the... he started the..."

"I know—I know, I caught him coming out of the house when I arrived." Damien was vague when he said, "I, uh... I handled him."

"No," I corrected. "No, not that fire. He started... the one that... the one before," I tried to explain. "It wasn't... it wasn't your father."

Damien's face twisted up in surprise. "He told you that?"

"He said he lit the match," I spoke through a seared esophagus. "Your father yelled at him, and he dropped it. There was gas everywhere. He still blames you, but—he's the one who lit the match. He told me this because he thought he was going to kill me, getting it off his chest because he thought I'd die with it."

Damien visibly cringed at that last statement.

"Morgan," he spoke my name regretfully, reaching for the side of my face with a single hand. It was then that I noticed the bandaging around my head. "I'm so sorry."

"Why are you sorry? You didn't do anything to me."

"He's my brother. My problem." I could feel his thumb caressing my cheek. "He could've killed you tonight."

"You ran into a burning building for me," I reasoned. How could I ever get mad at him now.

"Don't make it sound like some grand romantic gesture." Damien shook his head in disapproval. "It's the least I could've done considering..."

Brushing that off, I asked him, "Are you hurt anywhere?"

"No, the fire started in the kitchen where you were. You got the worst of it."

I lifted a hand to hold his fingers to my cheek. "Thank you for saving me."

"Don't thank me." Damien shook his head, and the air around him was exhausted. I wondered how much sleep he would've gotten in the two days I'd been in the hospital. "I'm the one who put you in that situation in the first place," he reminded.

"What did you do to Sebastien?"

"Don't worry about him," Damien replied swiftly. "Just know that he's never going to bother you again."

"Why? Is he in jail?"

Damien nodded.

"Did you beat him up?" I asked, hoping Damien would say he didn't. Not because I didn't think Sebastien deserved to be roughed up pretty bad, but because I knew Damien always laid hands on his brother against his better judgement. I wouldn't want Damien to do something awful to his brother that he would only regret later. If Sebastien was in police custody, that was good enough for me.

"I didn't have the time to beat him up," Damien answered regretfully. "My girlfriend was in a burning house."

"I couldn't move on my own," I told him, not wanting to seem like I simply resigned to dying without a fight. "The fire—I tried to move, but I—"

"You hit your head pretty hard, baby. I know. There was blood pooling in the foyer and underneath you when I found you," he explained. "It's a miracle that you're alive."

"Well, I'm alive because of you."

Damien frowned.

"You were in *danger* because of me," he rebuffed, grabbing hold of my hand. "But it'll never happen again."

"My house..." I whined regretfully after a short period of silence, remembering. "It's a pile of ash now, isn't it?"

"Not quite," Damien responded. "The kitchen and dining room need redoing. The rest of the house just needs a little cosmetic work done. You can stay with me while they fix it up."

My mind wandered to the month I spent living in Damien's apartment when we were first starting out. Oh how time had flown since then. If anyone had told me back then that this man would someday love me so much that he would charge into a burning house for me, I wouldn't have believed them at all.

"Do I get my old room back?" I tried not to smile.

"No." His grip on my hand tightened, his own smile budding faintly. There was a nostalgic glint in his eyes, as though he were recalling that first month together as well. Damien rose from his seat, pressing a kiss to my forehead before whispering, "I may never let you out of my sight ever again."

EPILOGUE

MORGAN

One month at Damien's apartment turned into one year.

We got comfortable, living together. Nobody had to leave to go see the other. We'd just wake up and there the other half was. Once we'd started, it was just too hard to stop. Even after my house was fixed, it sat empty for three months, before I simply decided to sell it.

Damien, of course, had no complaints. He'd wanted me to live with him all along, but it was I that had asked for separate living arrangements, so he honored it. Now, I couldn't bring myself to sleep alone, and he was all to willing to indulge me.

We were seated up against the headboard of our bed—him reading some emails, me reading a book. It was summer and for some internship experience before my final year of law school, I was interning in the law department of Damien's company.

It was nepotism to the highest degree, but I stopped fretting over my unfair advantage some time ago when I realized that I was going to marry Damien someday. No matter how much I tried to level the playing field, I was always going to be more privileged than my peers.

"How was your day at the office?" Damien's voice called me away from my book. "I think I might've heard about some trouble in legal."

"Oh, it wasn't trouble," I assured. "One of the staff members spilled her tea on my skirt, and she started crying, I think because she thought I'd try and get her fired."

"Hm," Damien considered this, pulling me in closer to him. "Was the tea hot?"

"It was *fine*," I assured, hearing that edge to his tone. He was not about to fire someone over an accident. "They already treat me like I'm you. What kind of intern sits at a desk all day? The only person who doesn't kiss my ass is the chief lawyer on the legal team, but that's probably only because he thinks you'll give me his job the second I pass the bar."

Damien's lips were in my hair, and I could feel the wind of his laugh warm my scalp. I could almost hear him rolling his eyes. "As if you would ever work for me."

"Right! I'm just gaining experience this summer so that I can go take my newfound talents to your competition someday. I wish they knew that."

"I wish *I* knew that," he muttered, but surely he knew that I was only joking.

"They treat me like I have the power to fire them at any moment. This is the most inauthentic internship experience ever. Nobody asks me to do anything!"

"You can pick up *my* coffee if you want to be treated like an intern so bad," Damien offered.

"What? So, everyone can see me walk into your office and think I'm giving you a nepotism blowjob?"

Damien sighed longingly at the thought.

I would never go into Damien's office at work. It bothered me that they all knew that I was the boss' girl. I definitely didn't want to remind them. We had never fooled around in his office and the only sign of privilege I chose to exhibit was the elevator I'd come in on.

"Sometimes I feel like I'm skating by. They must think I'm so damn unaccomplished."

Damien disagreed. "I happen to think you're very accomplished."

"I don't trust your opinion," I told him.

"Because I love you?"

"No because you're a freak of nature." He put his hand on his chest, pretending as if I'd hurt his feelings. "How do you even know what it looks like to be accomplished among normal people? We all probably look like ants from the heights you've ascended. God, you are a *billionaire*."

"And you *have* a billionaire. I think that's a little more impressive."

I couldn't help my smile then.

"Yes, you *are* mine," I agreed. "So, does that mean you'll do whatever I say?"

He smiled. "Sure."

"Mmmm," I tried to think of the most ridiculous thing I could ask for. "I think I want to change the name of the FINE building. What do you think of... The *Morgan* Building?"

"Shut *the fuck* up," he laughed, already going back on his word.

When the laughing subsided, I asked a real question. Something that had been on my mind heavily for a while now. "Are we always going to live here?"

"Here as in Miami or here as in this building?"

"This building. It's a little... cold sometimes. All the marble and sharp edges. At times, I feel like I'm living in an art installation."

Damien thought about it before he offered, "I can get us a house, if that's what you want."

"It is."

"Then make your demands, Mistress Morgan." I rolled my eyes at his continued usage of that name. He would always call me that when I'd ask for things, just before he'd oblige. He thought it was hilarious. It was our little inside joke.

"I want something seaside with a big grassy front yard, and the ocean in the back. Lots of windows. Two floors. A big eat-in kitchen where we can make and eat breakfast together, but also a formal dining room where we can eat at Thanksgiving, Christmas and on the kids' birthdays." He smiled at the last one. "Five bedrooms—one for us, three for the kids, and one for the guests."

"So, we're having three?" He mused fondly.

"Depends on how I feel about the first one. We shouldn't have more than one if the first one embarrasses me by looking like you."

He chuckled. "Fair enough."

I told him, "That's where I want to spend the rest of my life with you."

Damien pressed a kiss along my dimples, his hold around me tightening. "Consider it built."

One Year Later
Damien

Morgan held her twin sister's arm, telling her something I couldn't quite hear.

She looked stunning in her long pink dress, matching with the three other bride's maids standing at the front row.

Lauren was getting married today. Morgan was both her escort down the aisle and her maid of honor. Lauren's fiancé waited patiently at the altar, arms linked in front of him as Morgan walked and whispered.

When they passed my seat in the church, Morgan shot me a smile. Seeing Lauren in a wedding dress was disorienting. It was like seeing Morgan in a wedding dress, and the sight made the little black box in my pocket heavier.

The ceremony was long, but it passed quickly in my mind, drawing closer to my own moment of truth. Time flies so fast when you need it to slow down. Lauren said her vows, and her voice sounded so much like Morgan's, who stood behind her at the altar. I spent most of the ceremony, with my eyes glued on her.

Her hair was pulled back in an elegant style, curled at the sides. She was stunning up there. I couldn't wait to get her home so that I could ask her to be mine forever.

"You can have my sister back." Lauren pushed Morgan towards me after the cutting of the cake. By now, both women had changed out of their wedding clothes and into something more comfortable for the reception. They looked like they were wearing the same dress, but just different colors—white for Lauren, pink for Morgan. "She's starting to get on my nerves," Lauren explained.

The two had been fighting off and on since wedding preparations had begun. It was like watching Morgan bicker with herself. I thought it was cute. Morgan thought her and her sister were polar opposites, but it was easy to see the ways in which they were similar. For one, they both refused to back down from an argument. It made these past few months particularly turbulent.

"I'm ready to go home," Morgan announced as soon as Lauren was out of earshot. Tomorrow morning, one of them would cave and call the other and they'd cry on FaceTime about how much they loved each other.

But I would take Morgan up on that. As much as I liked Lauren, her wedding was filled with curious eyes that were also starting to weigh on me. It was part of the reason why I hated things like this—weddings. Just being surrounded by people who knew me as the guy who burned his mother alive.

The only person in the world who knew the whole truth was Morgan, a truth I might've never learned myself if not for my younger brother nearly killing her.

Sebastien was spending his next thirty years behind bars for what he tried to do to my girlfriend. To certain outsiders, it looked like he was, in a way, trying to avenge his mother's death. I allegedly killed his mother twenty years ago, so he was going to kill my girlfriend. That was the defense his public defender went with, trying to cop a temporary insanity plea.

When he got thirty years anyway, I noticed how much freer Morgan became, like his sentence lifted a weight off her shoulders. She was satisfied with thirty years of jail time. All I could think about was how he'd be out by the time he was fifty-four—if he didn't parole out sooner. He should've gotten more time.

"This isn't the way home." Morgan snapped me out of my thoughts on the car ride home, thinking I might've missed our exit.

I tried not to smile when I took my eyes off the road for a split second to tell her, "It is now."

We pulled up to a newly built white house near Key Biscayne, tucked away privately on a large plot of land. The yard out front was massive, lawn cut to perfection. A walkway cut down the middle, leading to a front door with half a dozen windows on either side.

Out back, you could hear the ocean crashing along the shore.

"Is this..." Morgan couldn't finish her sentence as she got out of the car. She walked up the walkway to the front door which was left unlocked for us. She let herself in, peeking into the empty house that smelled of new everything. "Is this the house that I asked for last ye—"

She was beginning to turn around, and behind her she found me—down on one knee.

Morgan immediately fell to the ground with me. It made me laugh a little bit. "You're not supposed to be on the ground with me, baby." I pulled the black box from my pocket. "Stand up so I can ask."

Morgan shook her head vehemently, telling me, "I want to be down here with you."

I tilted my head thoughtfully, accepting this as I opened up the box. "Morgan—"

"Yes," she answered before I could even finish. "Yes. Yes. A billion times yes! I'm yours."

And we sat there, both of us on the ground of our new empty house, neither of us above the other. Exactly how we liked it. We were a forever partnership.

Equals.

Made in the USA
Middletown, DE
28 May 2023

31636576R00137